Intrepid Paths—Burma

Melody Mociulski

Photo and illustration credits appear on page 148.

Cover design by Aye Myat Thu

ISBN 979-8-218-35443-5

To Michael and Tatiana
with infinity times love forever.

Contents

Prologue	7
Chapter 1—Burma 1974	14
Forced to Flee	27
Chapter 2—Burma 2010	44
Girls in Pink	48
Chapter 3—Burma 2011 and 2015	63
Delta Waters	70
Chapter 4—Burma 2016	84
Resilience	86
Chapter 5—Burma 2017	98
Standing Tall	100
Chapter 6—2021	116
The Choice	120
Chapter 7—Reflections	135
Acknowledgments	146
Image Credits	147

Everything Falls Away

*Sooner or later, everything falls away.
You, the work you've done, your successes,
large and small, your failures, too. Those
moments when you were light, alongside
the times you became one with the night.
The friends, the people you loved
who loved you, those who might have wished
you ill, none of this is forever. All of it is
soon to go, or going, or long gone.*

*Everything falls away, except the thread
you've followed, unknowing, all along.
The thread that strings together all you've
been and done, the thread you didn't know
you were taking until, toward the end,
you see that the thread is what stays
as everything else falls away.*

*Follow that thread as far as you can and
you'll find that it does not end, but weaves
into the unimaginable vastness of life. Your
life never was the solo turn it seemed to be.
It was always part of the great weave of
nature and humanity, an immensity we
come to know only as we follow our own
small threads to the place where they
merge with the boundless whole.*

*Each of our threads runs its course, then
joins in life together. This magnificent tapestry –
this masterpiece in which we live forever.*

—Parker J. Palmer

Myanmar's dictators changed the country's name from Burma to Myanmar in 1988. Many nations, including the United States, continue to refer to it as Burma, as does this author.

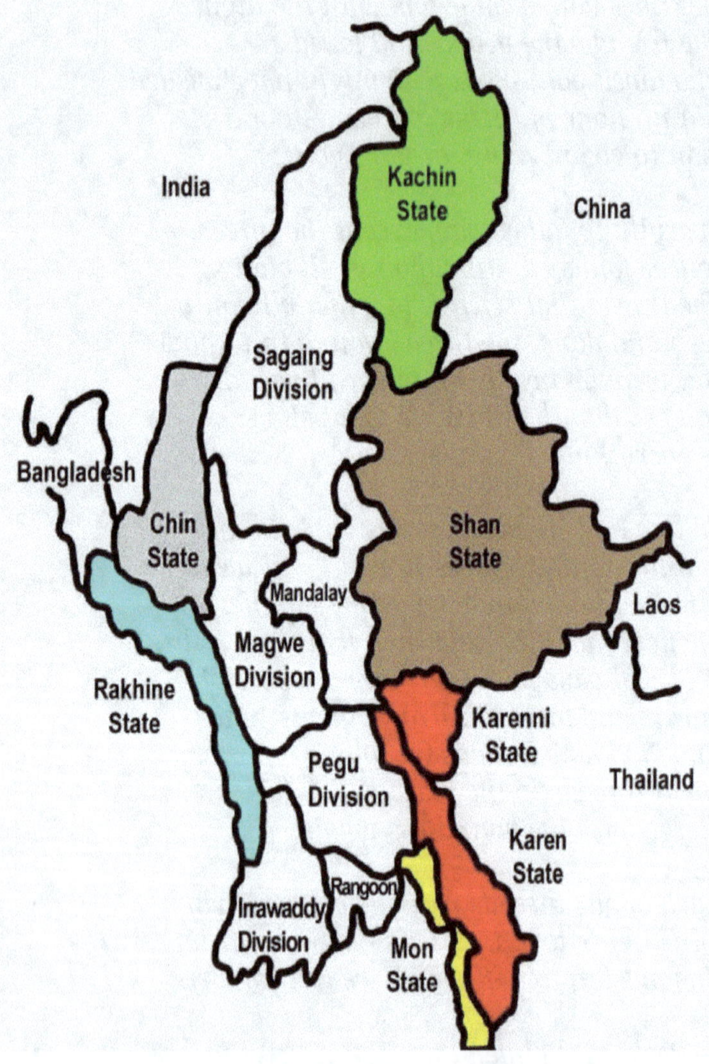

Burma 2022 Ethnic States Map

Prologue

Throughout my travels and life, I have never met people like the Burmese who are so willing to help others. If a woman has a dollar to her name, she will give half to another who might need it more. They have little, yet share with others. My friends and partners in Burma have demonstrated this over and over again. To see these intelligent, gifted, giving people brought to their knees with despair over the decades is heartbreaking.

Years ago, when I was going through a rough patch in my life, someone told me "life is not fair." Although hearing that at the time definitely didn't make me feel any better, I've never forgotten it. In today's world, we see endless examples of unfairness every day. The unfairness in Burma is merely one more, but it is the one that breaks my heart.

Burma is the largest Southeast Asia country, at 261,000 square miles. Bordered by China, Laos, Thailand, India, Bangladesh, the Andaman Sea, and the Bay of Bengal, and rimmed by mountain ranges to the north, east, and west, it is a land of lush hills, valleys, and the low-lying lands of the Delta region.

One of the beauties of Burma is the diversity of its population. Two-thirds of the population is Bamar—the ruling majority ethnic group for which the country was originally named. Of the 135 ethnicities in Burma, the predominate groups are Shan, Karen, Karenni, Mon, Kachin, Chin, and Arakanias. Each has its own state, unique language, dialects, customs, and folklore. Although Buddhism is the predominate religion, there is significant representation of Christians, Muslims, Hindus, and Nat worshipers throughout Burma.

In this book, I use the term Burmese broadly to represent all women of Burma, regardless of their ethnicity. No disrespect is intended.

Burma's history is mired in decades of repressive military junta rule, widespread poverty, and the world's longest-running ongoing civil wars with ethnic minority groups. It is known as one of the most brutal nations of all time for its mass human rights violations. In this book, for clarity, I refer to Burma's dictators as the military junta—a military or political group that rules a country after taking power by force.

The following provides a brief overview of Burma's political history.

1824–1948	British colonial rule
1948	Independence from British rule
1948–1962	Rule by Anti-Fascist People's Freedom League, instituting Buddhist socialism
1962	Ethnic rebel army formation in several ethnic states
1962–1988	Rule by Revolutionary Council headed by General Ne Win; military junta's closure of country by instituting severe visitation policy(maximum seven-days, entry and exit by plane)
1974	Burma's declaration as Socialist State
1987	Aung San Suu Kyi's prominence as protagonist for non-violent resistance against the dictatorial regime
1988	Military junta coup, establishing SLORC (State Law and Order Restoration Council)
1989	Renaming of Burma to Myanmar; renaming of capital (Rangoon) to

	Yangon; House arrest instituted for Aung San Suu Kyi, leader of the National League for Democracy (NLD)
1996	Foreign tourism initiated with Visit Myanmar Year 1996
2010	Military junta's voluntary dissolution in favor of officially endorsed civilian government, embedded within the legacy of the military junta's framework and networks,marred by corruption, money-laundering, and unrealistic projects
2021	Military junta's seizure of control via coup when first genuine democratic government was poised to convene
2024	Citizens' fight against military junta rule (The Spring Revolution) continues, some by peaceful protest and some by ethnic armed forces and People's Defense Force

Since 1962, the military junta has strictly controlled and censored all media. Because of this, citizens have limited knowledge of what is occurring throughout their own country. They do not know of battles between ethnic groups or genocides by and against certain groups. They do not know whether America is good or evil. They are afraid to ask questions for fear of obtaining knowledge that could harm them if arrested. Their ability to leave the country is extremely restricted. This is especially true for those without identity cards.

Many members of Burma's ethnic minorities, technically entitled to citizenship under the Citizenship Law, do not have identity cards, especially those living in areas that haven't been under government control for long periods of time. Access to written records, the difficulty of traveling to government-controlled areas for registration, and a general unwillingness of the government to register ethnic minorities make the process of proving citizenship immensely difficult. Without citizenship, they have no rights.

The 1982 Citizenship Law designated three categories of citizens: full citizens, associate citizens, and naturalized citizens. Only full and naturalized citizens are entitled to receive full rights of citizenship under the law. Associate citizens cannot own land or fixed property, cannot train to be doctors or engineers, cannot work for foreign firms, and cannot stand for any elected office.

Since my first connection with Burma in 1974 and my subsequent development of Educational Empowerment, I've strived to create awareness for Burma, its people, their struggles, and their triumphs.

This book is my tribute to Burmese women and girls—their incredible strength, resilience, perseverance, and potential. Though I've wanted to write it for a long time, I struggled with the best approach. I wanted a style that would be relatable to Westerners. One that would be factual. One that would provide the context for my connection to Burma. Big on research, I learned of an existing but unique format—the embedded narrative memoir. This option allowed me to protect the identities of my protagonists, to incorporate short fiction stories that would readily capture readers' attention, and to provide the backstory of my involvement with Burma and its people.

In writing these stories based on lives of women and girls known to me, I carry their faces in my mind—these women who entrusted me with their secrets. I feel a responsibility to accurately convey the restrictions under which they live—legal, political, cultural, economic, prejudicial, fear, and lack of access to basic rights. It's within these parameters that these women constantly demonstrate their strength.

Burmese women have the same values as women throughout the world. Their language, clothing, and living conditions may be different, but they seek the same things we all desire—honesty, community, freedom, justice, education, love, and security.

It's impossible to understate the impact we women have on each other. The power of our connections is echoed over and over again in our lives and in these stories. Whether it's mothers, sisters, friends or mentors, we listen, we encourage, and we support each other, even in the most desperate of moments.

The common threads throughout these stories are the unconventional life paths—often appearing when least expected, education's power to dramatically improve lives, and the value of women's support for each other. Obstacles and pathways vary, as do dreams. Yet, each of the protagonists demonstrates her steadfast determination to triumph.

I hope Intrepid Paths enables you to walk in the shoes of these women from the land of pagodas, to feel their pain, and to rejoice in their successes. I firmly believe that stories such as these build empathies. And isn't empathy what our chaotic world needs most today?

Thank you, in advance, for reading Intrepid Paths.

Chapter 1
Burma 1974

Even though it's been fifty years, her image is still embedded in my memory. She stands on the porch stoop, the early morning sun reflecting off her welcoming smile. Her lit cheroot cigar is as natural in her hand as a sixth finger. Her satiny longyi skirt drapes softly to the ground. Her expression invites connection, though no words are uttered.

She lives on the plateau of Bagan, home to thousands of Buddhist temples, where the vivid oranges and reds of the sunrises and sunsets reflecting off the stupas are legendary.

The year was 1974, my first sojourn into Burma. My partner (and later-to-be first husband) and I had been traveling for nine months through Eastern and Western Europe, the Mediterranean, Asia, and Southeast Asia.

We'd started in Amsterdam, purchasing a used, fully-equipped van, then travelled around, staying in campgrounds and exploring little-known sites. Finally arriving in Greece, we sold the van and continued our journey via public transport. In Istanbul, we met a British guy with an old Mercedes bus. He provided month-long transport from Istanbul to Kabul, Afghanistan. We joined his existing bus-load of long-haired hippie guys and slowly jostled across Turkey and Iran. Arriving on the western border of Afghanistan at Herat late at night was like stepping back in time. Light from lanterns. Men riding horseback with white robes billowing behind them. Roadway market stalls a hubbub of activity. A moment to remember.

Unbeknownst to us initially, most of our bus companions were heading to Kandahar in southern Afghanistan to score hashish. Luckily, none were caught and arrested. By the time we arrived in Kabul, we were relieved to say goodbye to our new acquaintances.

Onward once again through Pakistan to Kashmir. At that time, in-country fighting in Kashmir was minimal and foreign travelers were allowed entrance. Taking a week-long journey with a local multi-generational family up the Jhelum River to Dal Lake was breathtaking. Papa propelling the punt boat. Grandma relaxing with tea and her hookah. Mama and toddler smiling shyly at us. Oyster pink clouds lighting the morning skies. Absolutely sublime.

Back to India and onward to Nepal for trekking to Mt. Everest base camp. In those days, travelers journeyed up from Australia and New Zealand towards Europe. We were taking the opposite route toward Bali to experience the much-touted dancing maidens, magic mushrooms, and fruit salads.

Fellow travelers were our only source of news updates and advice—countries to see, routes to take, places to avoid. While in Katmandu, we learned that Burma allowed entry by plane for a maximum stay of seven days. Although we knew little of Burma, we decided it was an opportunity not to be missed.

We arrived in Rangoon in January 1974 and sought out the YMCA for lodging. Since we weren't married, we weren't allowed to share a room. My partner bedded down in the spacious men's dormitory—platform bed frames, screened windows, overhead fans. The women's "dormitory" was a tiny room—no furniture, one window with no screen, no overhead fan. Mosquitos were plentiful and aggressive. Although each of us residents tried to keep our heads covered as protection from the critters, it was impossible. We all awoke with swollen faces and tired eyes.

Walking the next morning through the broad streets of Rangoon, lined with squat Victorian buildings, we found an open market selling fresh food, clothing, and crafts. As we both carried only one large backpack during our year-long journey, shopping opportunities were limited. However, when I found a jade bangle, I knew it was going back home with me. (I eventually gifted it to my daughter who continues to wear it.)

During this period, Rangoon's diplomatic community comprised the majority of foreigners in the city. The local art scene expanded noticeably. Severe economic regulations restricted foreign imports. Censorship ruled.

Later we would hear of students and workers roaming these streets in December 1974, setting fire to public buildings—violence that erupted in response to the military junta's refusal to give General U Thant a state funeral. Martial law was declared in Rangoon. The rest of the country was already governed by a special law one step removed from martial law.

Our visas only allowed travel outside of Rangoon to either Mandalay or Bagan. We eagerly decided to see Bagan, having heard of the 10,000 pagodas and religious sites. The next day, we boarded a Burma Airways turboprop plane with trepidation. All went well. We soon touched down in Bagan, which sits on a bend of the Irrawaddy River in the central plains of Burma. An oxen-drawn cart took us along a dirt-covered road to a thatched roof hut that would be our lodging for the next three nights. We were literally surrounded by hundreds upon hundreds of brick-red and honey-colored cone-shaped pagodas.

Our days in this majestic and isolated setting were magical and peaceful. Rising early with the sun, we wandered aimlessly through fields of pagodas. We had them all to ourselves while birds swirled around the rooftops and howling mongrels looked for food. Walking to the river, we watched fishermen throwing their nets out for the day's harvest and laden ox carts pulling loads across the Irrawaddy. We found a small eatery for breakfast meals of fried rice topped with fried egg. It was here that I saw the woman on the stoop—where we looked into each other's eyes with curiosity. We didn't speak. We didn't turn away. We held each other's attention. To this day, I think of her and wish I had learned her story.

The aura of Bagan and that fleeting connection with the woman on the stoop have sat deep within my heart all these years. I know in my soul that it was the catalyst leading me to founding my nonprofit, Educational Empowerment (EE), thirty-eight years later to support women in Burma.

As a twenty-seven years old woman, literally traveling the world, I had a curious outlook but little knowledge of the history, culture, or people of the countries we traversed.

I was a passive observer of the wonders and mysteries appearing before my eyes in these faraway lands. Living in the moment, I empathized with the pain and joy of the people I encountered. Yet there were no visceral connections until Bagan and the Burmese woman on the stoop. I have often wondered why that was different. Was it unique to a bond between women that transcends borders, languages, ages, and skin colors? Was it the magic of Bagan and its spiritual aura? Was it all that and more? What I do know is that I did not experience anything else like it throughout our travels. Burma was exceptional.

Although I wasn't aware of this at that time, I have always instinctively been drawn to women of other cultures—their challenges, their fears, their destinies. I have always believed that we women can change our world for the better, if only we're given the opportunity and the skills.

Over the years, I have learned to be open to new possibilities, some more obvious than others and some taking longer to realize than expected. I have learned to not tie myself rigidly to a plan, which can mean inadvertently missing other opportunities. I have learned that the unsought path is often the better choice. When I open myself to new paths, I never know where life will take me.

One of my first life experiences in choosing the unknown path occurred when I was working for the City of Seattle in my thirties. I half-heartedly scanned the classifieds one Sunday morning. A relatively vague job posting referenced a need for experience with government-funded employment programs for low-income youth. This closely matched my position at the time. Open to change, I submitted my application and soon received a call inviting me for an interview in Manhattan. Although my parents believed I would be abducted if I fell for the apparent "scam," I packed my bag and headed to New York for the first time.

Arriving at the hotel on Park Avenue where a room had been reserved for me, I was unexpectedly upgraded to a suite on the top floor. I had never entered a hotel suite, let alone used one exclusively, and I was so excited that I opened the window (this was back when hotel windows opened), stuck my head out, and yelled "Hello, New York!" I then found the nearest deli and ordered a pastrami sandwich.

The position was legitimate. I was offered the job as an out-stationed representative for Manpower Development Research Corporation (MDRC), which monitored and evaluated government-funded employment programs for low-income youth.

As soon as I returned home, I resigned my position with the City and began establishing an office in downtown Seattle. My assigned geographic radius for monitoring existing programs included all of King and Snohomish counties, as well as special assignments in Berkeley and Detroit. Ford Foundation provided MDRC with the funding for all out-stationed personnel. Much to my delight, this included monthly staff meetings in Manhattan, providing the unanticipated benefit of exploring New York's shopping, theatre, and dining options.

My role with MDRC afforded me invaluable confidence-building experience—writing, analyses, communication, and travel. It taught me that "it never hurts to ask" and to "step outside the box." It also provided me with insight into the struggles, needs, and potential of young people in my own country. This was a valuable lesson in learning to listen to my instincts and being open to change.

When the MDRC project with the government was completed, I was given the choice of moving to Manhattan or taking a layoff. I chose the layoff, and, several months later, gave birth to my beautiful daughter Tatiana. After a planned year of stay-at-home motherhood, it was time to jump back into the workforce.

Thinking that the private sector afforded me the most potential for upward mobility and income, I accepted a position in a management training program with Seattle-First National Bank. Two months later, a devastating banking disaster occurred, and my management training program was axed. I was faced with the decision to settle for a secretarial position with Seattle-First or to once again hit the streets looking for employment. By that time, I was a single mom. I was afraid to move to another employment option. How long would it take? Would I find anything? I decided to become a secretary once again, staying at the bank.

Looking back, this is an example of my not seeking the unknown path—rather, staying with the known. I soon realized that I was bored and underutilized at Seattle-First. After several months of dissatisfaction, I began looking for alternative employment and soon found a position as a financial analyst with City of Seattle's Engineering Department. It was one of the best moves I could have made—excellent upward mobility and income, job security, and eventually a significant monthly pension.

After officially retiring from City of Seattle in 2004 at age fifty-seven, with pension in hand and time to do whatever caught my interest, I enjoyed the freedom to work or not. A local travel store hired me as a part-time staff, and it was great fun to hear others' travel tales and share mine with them. Next, I accepted a part-time office position with the local Waldorf school. My favorite responsibility there was greeting the children outside in the morning and ringing the bell when it was time for school to begin.

In 2007, I turned sixty and found myself feeling a need to push my comfort levels and prove to myself that I could still be self-reliant. A friend shared with me her stories and photos from volunteering at an elephant-rescue sanctuary in Northern Thailand. Next thing I knew, I was heading off to Chiang Mai by myself, with a full backpack assembled for a three-week volunteer adventure.

There were thirty elephants—moms, aunties, babies, sisters, and two males—Max, largest bull elephant in Thailand, and Big K, who sported one glorious tusk. It was rustic and magical—feeding them, bathing them in the river, watching their antics and soap-opera stories play out.

Before being rescued to live at the sanctuary, they'd suffered heart-wrenching torture in the name of breaking their spirits so they would perform tricks for tourists. But now they were free!

Since I was the birthday girl, I was given "the palace" for my lodging—actual bed, personal toilet, and a bright purple mosquito net. I felt totally special, even though my new Brit friend Harvey chided me mercilessly as he trotted off to his mat on the floor of his shared dorm room.

Regular duties included poop scooping, corn shucking, fruit hauling, and, the best, feeding the elephants. Nothing like the succulent slurping sounds an elephant makes while curling her trunk around freshly shucked corn, ready to pop into her mouth.

The elephants' sense of family, playfulness, and appreciation for the freedom to simply be was a gentle reminder of the beauty surrounding me.

Vivid memories: Sitting outside on my veranda in the stifling afternoon humidity, coffee in hand, elephant caretaker mahoots playing guitar and singing in the background, birds providing accompaniment. Being stinky and filthy after a day's work. Never happier.

This was the first of what would become many ventures to Southeast Asia and other confidence-building experiences. Once again, I learned that I could take risks and survive. Seeing how others in the world live taught me to appreciate all that I have home in the States and reminded me that worldly belongings are not the basis for happiness.

Upon returning home from Chiang Mai, additional volunteering seemed the next logical step. Now eager to explore the vast world, I shied away from local community volunteer opportunities and sought out international options.

One afternoon, a classified ad in the local tabloid seeking volunteer support for an international nonprofit organization caught my eye. Clear Path International (CPI) provided support to landmine-accident survivors in Afghanistan and Southeast Asia. It turned out that my new neighbor was the founder and director of CPI. Another unexpected path had opened to me.

Before I knew it, I was loading cargo containers of wheelchairs, walkers, and crutches for delivery to Vietnam. This quickly blossomed into an opportunity to work for pay as CPI's Southeast Asia Program Director, managing operations in Cambodia, Laos, Vietnam, Thailand, and Burma. Travel had been a priority in my life since my teen years. This job, encompassing support to others and travel to far-flung locations, seemed like my dream come true.

Annual trips to Southeast Asia commenced. My connections with women of other cultures grew exponentially. Finally, I was able to learn first-hand what women in these lands hoped for and struggled to achieve. I saw how women throughout the world instinctively supported each other—through listening, laughing, encouraging, and crying together.

I found myself drawn to the stories of women living in Burma, families fleeing through jungles seeking safety to reach refugee camps across the border in Thailand. Camps providing sanctuary, food, shelter, and education for the youth. Camps with overcrowding, chaos, food shortages, sanitation problems, and a cage-like atmosphere that took its toll as families waited in the hope of being resettled someday.

One young girl's memories of fleeing for safety resonated deeply with me.

That Day

I remember that day,
of sadness.
Black pigs were hungry,
cried for food.
Tiny yellow chicks
Looked for their mother.
Dogs tried to find their owners,
to feel they were not alone.

Young people left school to work,
and came home without money.
They came home
with the smell of sweat on their foreheads.
Young people left their family
because of money.
Money is so important,
almost like it will bring
a feeling of heaven.
But the little money they made
could not provide for their lives.
It broke their families apart.

I remember that day
of family time.
Fathers left
their wives and children behind,
to find food,
to find sustenance.

But soon
families without fathers
became like the rainbow missing color
and like fish without
clear fresh water in the river.

Kids were without dads,
the smell of happiness
was gone.
Like the wind
carrying the smoke of food away,
the light heart of a mother and child
became heavier.

If only everyone was
with their family that day
and not separated,
the world would just be
colorful as today.
And there will be no more
that day.

—Phen Meh

Forced to Flee

I never tire of this view. The sun sinking slowly into the sloping rolling hills of bamboo, enriching the countryside with its intense purple haze. Birds calling out to their babies, "Mama will be home soon with your dinner, little ones." For these brief moments, I'm able to shut out the chaos and noise of the camp surrounding me—the camp that has been my home for the past seven years.

I was only four years old in 1997 when that day turned my world upside down. That day when Mama, Papa, and I fled our real home in the Karenni State. I still carry vivid images floating around in my head. The flames erupting throughout our village as the military junta burnt it to the ground. Mama scolding me to drop my toys and run as fast as a bunny. Children screaming. Grandmas crying. Gunshots filling the air. My heart pounding as if to burst. The Karenni countryside plunging into terror.

I remember walking for hours after we fled our village. My feet burned with pain and my belly grumbled with hunger. We found a hidden spot in the forest to rest. I fell asleep quickly, exhausted from the trauma and the journey. When we awoke at daylight, we started walking once again. At last, we crossed the Thailand border near Ban Mai Nai Soi, a Karenni refugee camp.

The camp's entry gates were big enough to allow cars and trucks to enter. Barbed wire, strung onto the gate posts, ran as far as my eyes could see in both directions. I saw children on the other side of the fence playing and staring at us. Outside the gates, families, looking tired and weak, waited to speak to the guards. When it was our turn, the guard told us that 20,000 Karenni people lived in the camp. I thought that seemed like too many people. Only 10,000 people lived in our home village.

The guard told Mama and Papa we needed to build our own bamboo house. He gave us a temporary hut for sleeping that night. With trepidation, we walked through the gates. Would we be safe here? Would there be enough food? Would people welcome us?

Once inside, other families saw our exhausted faces and bodies. They showed us to our temporary hut and where to find water by the river. They gave us some of their rice to eat. I could see that Mama and Papa were thankful for this kindness. I was too tired and hungry to think much beyond food and sleep, but I was also curious about this new village. I saw children playing ball, mamas cooking, papas smoking pipes and talking. I heard Mama's Kay Ba dialect and Papa's Kayah dialect. That made me feel at home a bit. But this village looked nothing like our real home.

Our first morning in the camp, Papa and Mama started building our house on a tiny spot of land in the sea of homes. They cut and carried bamboo from the surrounding jungle. I helped by collecting leaves for the roof. It didn't take us long to finish the house. It was only one big room with a thatched roof and no door or windows, but it was ours.

Camp leaders and international aid workers brought us bedding and floor mats, pots, and water jugs. They told us to be careful on the walkways as many were rickety. They warned us that toilets were always falling apart because of the tropical climate and heavy usage.

People in the camp used rainwater for drinking and bathing. We pickled bamboo shoots and foraged for wild greens to supplement our diet of rationed rice. We learned that some young people snuck out illegally to work for a week or two to help support their families. Within the camp, people sold small things like snacks, books, or playing cards. They used money earned for basics.

Our family is Christian. But all religious groups, including animists, Muslims, and Buddhists were represented in the camp and had their own places of worship. We soon learned that the camp was run by the refugees who lived there—teachers, religious leaders, medics, water and sanitation workers, trash collectors, and shopkeepers. These groups were much like those in our home village. This felt familiar.

The women's organizations served as the glue binding our camp life together. They watched out for children's welfare, and took care of the most vulnerable people—widows, victims of abuse, and orphans. Most refugees usually felt better once they arrived at the camp after their long traumatic journeys. When people lost everything, finding sanctuary, food, and shelter was an immense relief.

It wasn't until years later that Papa explained to me why we had to leave our village and come to Thailand.

"Nang, you're old enough now for me to tell you why we left our home. The military junta wanted our land where rice grew fast and well. They planned to move us to the high mountains in the north. But I knew that the land in that valley wouldn't be good for growing our crops. We wouldn't find water as in our village where the river runs swift and sure. Our paddy fields would fail, and we would go hungry.

"Unfortunately, some of our friends from the village did go to the mountain camps. A couple of my friends eventually escaped and told me what it was like. They were all crowded into overflowing trucks, rank with still air. The long bumpy drive was unending. Thousands of people were moved there. Many died from hunger. Many were forced to work on the railway or to be unpaid laborers for the military junta, building roads, clearing land, or carrying weapons. Children were also forced to work. No one was allowed to leave camp. If they did, they might be shot on sight."

"I'm so thankful that you knew not to go there, Papa," I sighed with relief. "But it makes me sad for our friends who ended up there."

"Yes, Nang, it's heartbreaking and shows the evilness of the military junta. Some of our villagers who didn't go to the mountain camp decided to live in the forests. They saw the military junta plant landmines in our paddy fields to prevent us from returning to farm our lands and knew it would be impossible to return to their crops. In the forest, they ate whatever they could find. Many nearly died from poisonous plants. They made simple huts or slept under banana leaves for fear of being discovered, because if the soldiers found their huts or small crop fields, they burned them down.

"Even big cities such as Loikaw were devastated by the military junta—bombs were dropped by fighter jets and access to water was blocked. Battles between resistance fighters and the military junta grew worse each day. Some people in Loikaw stayed to protect their homes from thieves. Others were stranded in monasteries. Others weren't physically able to travel. The military junta randomly arrested people and kept them in prison indefinitely."

"Why is the military junta so wicked, Papa?" I asked.

"I believe it's because they're greedy. They want our lands, gems, and minerals."

"But aren't we all just people like you and Mama—kind, hardworking, peaceful?" I asked. "Why can't everyone get along and share?"

"I don't know, sweet daughter. I wish it were so."

"When your Mama and I heard these horrifying stories, we knew that life in our serene little village would never return. We knew that the military junta would always be at war with us."

"So, we decided to flee into Thailand and find a Karenni refugee camp. It was our only choice. Your freedom and safety was our first priority."

"Oh, Papa. I love you and Mama over the moon," I said, giving him a big hug. "Thank you for saving us!"

Remembering our first taste of refugee life at Ban Mai Nai Soi Camp, my face crinkles into a smile. My little brother Chul was born one year after our arrival. He brings such a gift of joy and hope to our family. Ever since he was a tiny baby, he has followed me everywhere. I turn around and there he is, just like my shadow. He looks to me to learn Mama's and Papa's dialects. If he is sad, he turns to me for a comforting squeeze. If he is excited, he runs to me on his chubby little legs to tell me the news.

Mama and Papa are always busy and tired from chores and obligations in the camp. It's assumed that Chul is my responsibility, but I don't mind. He always lights up my face.

When I was little in our real village, Mama told me folktales—stories that her Mama had told her. Now I share these Karenni folktales with Chul so he will know about our heritage. My first story for Chul was my favorite, The Journey of the Kayah People in Papa's dialect.

The story tells of the original Kayah people living at the top of the highest mountain in Karenni State. Every year they celebrated a festival called Ta-Ya-I-Lu, honoring all Kayah ancestors.

After living on the beautiful mountaintop for many years, they left in search of better land and water. It was difficult to find such a good place. One night in the darkness, they ran into a big rock wall, blocking them from moving forward. They tried many things to break through the wall. First, silver-horned horses. The wall didn't crack, but their horns broke. That's why horses don't have horns to this day. Next, an elephant. He wasn't successful, nor was the buffalo whose horns bent and became forever curved.

Feeling disappointed, they prayed to the guardian spirit to help solve their problem. The guardian sent an armadillo that kept biting at the wall. Finally, there was a crack and the wall crumbled down! The armadillo lost all his teeth and couldn't eat. He asked the guardian spirit to find food for him. The guardian spirit told him to search in the soil. Ever since then, armadillos have eaten bugs and termites.

The people rushed through the rubble of the wall. Some of their animals came with them: the rooster to make predictions for the Kayah, the cat to protect humans from evil spirits, the dog to serve the spirits, the buffalo to help with farming, and the elephant and the horse to carry heavy loads and build homes.

Finally, the Kayah arrived at a big lake called Nos. It became their home.

The Kayah wanted to celebrate their festival of Ta-Ya-I-Lu again. The guardian spirit told them to set up their bamboo poles in daytime and celebrate the festival at night. To this day, this is how the Kayah celebrate Ta-Ya-I-Lu.

Chul's big blue eyes beamed as he listened quietly to the folktale. "Is this story true, Nang?" he asked.

"I like to think so," I replied. "The Karreni people are strong, resilient, and determined. We believe in guardian spirits. They help us in our lives, especially when we have problems. As you grow up, remember that our guardian spirits are always with us, protecting us."

As Chul and I grew up inside this camp, we saw good things and bad things. We were surrounded by other Karenni people, speaking our same dialects. We understood what was being said. Foods cooked over the campfires were familiar and tempting. Camp residents said that food was our social "talk," binding us together. We felt relatively secure and safe from the wars. We developed rich friendships with other children and families.

The biggest positive, though, was access to education. Our camp teachers taught us to read, in both Karenni dialects and Burmese. We had a makeshift library with books donated by support agencies. Chul and I spent hours sitting outside together, reading our books, transporting us to faraway make-believe worlds filled with smiles and love.

However, there were also bad things about refugee life. Some we learned on our own and others we learned while sitting around firesides with elders.

Illegal drugs permeated the camp. Girls, tasked with gathering firewood, were easy prey for assault when venturing out at dawn for breakfast fires. Hidden landmines, prevalent in fields surrounding the camp, posed a high risk of death or loss of limbs for anyone venturing outside the camp.

Some parents beat their children and some husbands their wives, as camp life created pressure within families. Some refugees felt mentally trapped by camp life and turned to suicide for escape. Privacy in the camp was impossible.

Although education was provided, it was very limited in scope. We didn't learn English. We didn't have options for higher education.

The refugee camp felt like limbo. We couldn't go forward, and we couldn't go back. We were homeless people, stateless people, who had lost everything. Most of us at some point felt destitute, humiliated, and helpless.

One morning my sweet friend Ming expressed her anger about life as a refugee:

Living in the camp
we are like a wild cat
that is being raised in domesticity.
Cannot get out of the cave.
We are like an offender
who is punished.
We do not have freedom.
We cannot do as we wish.

For me, a sense of community and a link to my Karenni culture is the identity that I crave and fear losing. Many people from our village made it to the camp and we try to live together in the same section of the camp. Even though we lost our homes, sharing time with old neighbors makes refugee life a bit more bearable.

Our cultural identity is linked to our crafts. We're very proud of our intricate silver jewelry, brass neck rings, lacquerware, traditional clothing, and homemade rice wine served in clay jars. I worry that will be lost if we stay in the camp too long. We don't have the space or time to perform our traditions or reveal our true selves. It worries me that our culture is fading away. I wrote this poem to express my worries and emotions:

Imagine

Imagine, in the future
what will our Karenni State
become?

Will we still have
our mother's custom and
our father's place?

Imagine, in the future
who will our Karenni youth become?
Will our language and literature still exist?

Imagine, in the future
who will our future generations become?
Will love, peace, and freedom remain with them?

Imagine.

We have lived in Ban Mai Nai Soi Camp for six years—day after day with little change.

At ten years old, I'm still not sure what I look like. There are very few mirrors in the camp, so I haven't seen a reflection of myself since we arrived here. I see Papa as handsome, tall and strong, with a happy smile that lights up when he sees Chul and me. Mama as short and slim with beautiful blue eyes. Others in the camp call her stunning. My parents tell me I'm beautiful with my long thick black hair and enormous brown eyes. I assume they just say that because they love me. Chul, a big boy of six, is already gaining on me in height. Quick to smile, with an easy demeanor, he is a favorite amongst his playmates.

One night at the campfire, Mama and Papa tell us that many in camp are considering possible resettlement to America. It requires application and could take a long time to hear about approval, or not. Some camp residents' family members or friends are already resettled. They have written letters about their challenges in moving to such an enormous country as America.

Just like our decision to flee Karenni State and our opinions of living in this camp, there are upsides and downsides to resettlement. Some residents are determined to stay in the camp. They don't want to face the upheaval of going abroad, or they hope to return to their village again someday, or they need to stay to take care of elders.

"I've heard there have been many divorces in the camp," Mama tells us. "The mamas want to resettle, believing a better future awaits their children in America. The papas want to stay in the camp, believing they will eventually be able return to Burma. Families torn apart with mamas taking the children to America and papas staying in the camp."

"Our minimal ability to speak English would be our biggest challenge for life in America," Mama shares. "One of my friends told me her daughter resettled last year. She remained house-bound, afraid to go out, fearing she would have to speak to people. Another woman ventured outside but wandered for days. She didn't know her address nor how to ask for help in English. And a young Karenni woman with three children called the social welfare office after living in America for only a few weeks, asking to be allowed to return to the camp. She didn't believe she could ever acclimate to the complex life of America."

Hearing these stories, I feel pain for my family and all the camp residents. We've all experienced unbelievable traumas. We've all dreamed of a better future but know that dreams don't always come true. We've all feared another move to an unknown land. And we don't know what to expect—either here or in America.

Another night Papa calls out to Chul and me. "Let's sit by the fire and discuss together whether to stay in the camp or apply for resettlement to America. You children are still young, but it's important for you to share your feelings. I don't want our family to break apart. We must agree unanimously whether to go or to stay."

"Okay, Papa", says Chul holding my hand tightly and snuggling in close to Mama.

"As I told you before," says Papa, "I've always wanted this camp life to be temporary. We've been here six years now, and it doesn't look hopeful that events in Burma will improve. There's still much fighting, and the greedy military junta doesn't seem willing to give up its position. I'm not hopeful that our Karenni State will ever again be safe for us."

"Chul, you were born in this refugee camp. You've never seen a town or city. For this camp to be the only world you know is a heartbreaking thought for me. I see your strength and curiosity about life. My hope for you and Nang is bigger than this camp."

"Nang, you're becoming a woman. You are very bright. I fear a life for you in this camp would mean marrying early, becoming a mother, and never experiencing the outside world."

"Mama, please tell us your thoughts," says Papa.

"I agree with all you've said, Papa. I've always believed in hope. I don't think we should stay here complacently waiting for good things to appear. We need to be brave and find a new path—one where we can live freely, where we can find a Karenni community in America, and where we can thrive. I know it won't be easy. It will be an unknown. But my heart tells me it is a risk worth taking," says Mama with a sparkle in her eyes. "All right, children, it's your turn to speak. Nang, you go first."

I don't hesitate. "I want to go to college and become a teacher or a scientist or an engineer. I want to be safe. I want more food to eat. I want to climb mountains with friends and have my own bedroom. I want many things that aren't available here in a refugee camp. I want to be a Karenni American," I declare. "I am also afraid, but I'm willing to face my fears for freedom—to think what I want, say what I want, and do what I want."

Chul chimes in with a resounding "Yes! I want all those things too, Nang. Camp life is boring, sad, and the same thing every day. I'm willing to take the chance of resettling. Okay, it will probably be very hard at times. But it's hard here also. So, why not? What do we have to lose?"

"Thank you, Mama, Nang, and Chul for honestly sharing your feelings," says Papa. "It sounds to me like we have a decision! I will visit the Camp Director's office tomorrow to start the resettlement application process. I'll tell you everything I learn about our chances of being resettled. I love each of you so much and am very proud of your strength and courage."

Papa completes the paperwork the next day. And then the waiting period begins. It is excruciating to awake every morning, hoping for good news and not hearing a peep. Life in the camp continues in the same routine. Time moves slowly. All we can do is wait.

After a year, the Camp Director seeks out Papa to share the good news: We've been approved for resettlement to America. We leave next week!

Each of us will receive a one-time grant as "welcome" money. It will be approximately 1,000 US-dollars each and will be essential help for rent and household needs until Mama and Papa find work.

We'll be moving to Washington State on the west coast of America. We don't know anything about that state nor what to expect. When we arrive, we'll be met by social workers who will help us get settled temporarily.

We don't have many belongings, as most were left in our village and camp life is meager. However, we each receive one bag to pack our clothing and special memory items.

We start our rounds of goodbyes to friends in the camp. It's difficult to be the ones leaving, but we're happy to be the ones going.

The day is here! It's June 20, 2004, a day to remember. We're part of a large group waiting near the camp's entry gate. Soon, a bus will take us to the airport and then onward to America.

The air today is hot and more stifling than usual. I see others waiting for the bus, their wrists adorned with thick bands of white string, symbolizing peace, harmony, good fortune, and good health as we head out for our journey to freedom.

While we wait, Chul and I are given sunglasses. We've never owned such things. "Look at me, Nang. Do I look handsome with my sunglasses?" giggles Chul.

"Oh my, yes you do, little brother," I laugh.

I see so many emotions in the eyes of the others crowded around us. This is a big day. It brings sadness from leaving the familiar, fear of flying on an airplane, nervousness of entering a country of which we know little, and hope for a better life.

I poke Chul and ask, "What are you most excited about, little man?"

"The airplane—flying in the clouds like a bird, looking down below us at the countries and the oceans!" exclaims Chul.

"How about you, Mama?"

"I'm excited to have some space all to myself and quiet moments of peace," says Mama solemnly.

"And you, Papa? What are you most looking forward to?" I ask.

"I'm very happy and relieved to know that each of you will be safe. I'm especially excited that you and Chul will have access to a good education," says Papa proudly. "What about you Nang?"

"I learned from one of the social workers that there are many mountains in Washington State. I'm excited to see them and climb to their heights. Maybe they will look like the mountains in our Karenni State. That would be wonderful!" I say with a big smile. "Mostly though, I'm very thankful to be with you, Mama, and Chul. I know it will be easier for me to remain strong in facing the unknowns of this new country if we're all together.

"I will always love my homeland, my beautiful Karenni State, the place where I was born. I will work hard to be worthy of this new opportunity. I will always remember that I am Karenni, and I will do all I can to keep my Karenni identity alive."

It's time to enter the bus. I take one last look at the bamboo-covered hills and say, "Please lead the way for us, Papa."

Chapter 2
Burma 2010

During one trip along the Thailand–Burma border in 2010, my Burmese friend and colleague offered to take me up into the hills to Loi Tai Leng, a displaced-person camp for families impacted by landmine accidents. Although the narrow, bumpy, cliff-edge ride kept my heart pounding for endless hours, the ultimate destination was breathtaking. Seeing the families, impacted by loss of limbs, homes, and income-generating options was humbling.

I awoke early the next day to explore the village and catch the early morning light for photos and happened upon a young Burmese woman with her wide-eyed daughter strapped to her back. As we stared at each other and smiled, I felt that connection again—woman to woman. Although I didn't know her story, I knew her life was difficult—displaced, living in chronic poverty, and victim to ongoing abuses enacted by the military junta. Yet in that moment her welcoming smile conveyed a sense of joy. I wondered how she could be happy when she had so little. In her, I saw the power of the human spirit to continue to hope for a better life, even in the face of despair.

That woman in that moment was another turning point for me. I realized that I wanted to help her and all the women and girls in her country attain their rights for a better life. Although I had been learning to listen to my heart, I had not yet consciously created a new path to follow. This was the impetus for that new path.

Though I was extremely grateful for the opportunity to help landmine-accident survivors receive medical support and income-generating work, and I felt honored to have contributed to this worthy effort, when meeting with CPI beneficiaries, especially those in Vietnam, I felt like an intruder invading their space to view their trauma. As if the beneficiaries were being paraded in front of me. I was never comfortable, and I don't believe they were either. I empathized with their pain, but I did not relate to them personally.

I did know, however, that education stirred my heart. And I believed that education could help women like the young mother in Loi Tai Leng.

In 2011, I was able to obtain a small grant for CPI from the US State Department for an education project inside Burma. The State Department was already CPI's primary donor, especially for Afghanistan and Vietnam. The funding for Burma was a one-off grant to scope out the country's landscape, given the political climate.

I learned from my Burmese connections that many children received an education at Buddhist monasteries and nunneries. Even though government schools were technically free, poor families couldn't afford to purchase the school uniforms or provide gratuities to the teachers, necessary to ensure their children received adequate attention. Monks and nuns were willing to provide classroom education for these families free of charge. Their approach to education was much more comprehensive than that provided in the government schools and included development of problem-solving skills. Government schools' approach focused on memorizing answers to annual exam questions.

Although well intentioned, teachers in the monastic and nunnery schools were not well trained. With minimal education themselves, they were inadequately prepared to motivate, educate, and nurture the minds of children, especially children who were victims of poverty, inequitable opportunities, and, often, domestic violence.

In the monastic and nunnery schools all grades were crowded together in one large room. Noise levels could be so extreme that students and teachers couldn't hear each other. Supplies for both teachers and students were nearly non-existent.

Our Burmese connections recommended specific monastic and nunnery schools where we could focus our support to provide teacher-training and classroom materials. They accompanied us on site visits to translate and provide background stories of the students' circumstances.

This project was my first step in Burma to empower women and students with education.

Girls in Pink

"No, Mama, don't leave me and Thiri," I sob, hanging onto her legs for dear life. "Why are we here? Are these women nuns? Is that why they're all wearing pink robes? It's cold and dirty in this big building. And there are so many other girls. Some are crying and looking sad. What is happening?"

"Aye Sander and Thiri, this is where you are going to live now," whispers Mama. "You will be safe here. The nuns will be kind and take good care of you. You and your sister will be together, and you will be taught to read. You've been wanting to learn your alphabet, right?"

"No, Mama, that isn't important," I cry. "We want to be with you and Papa. We promise to be good girls for you. We won't fight anymore. We just want to go home."

"You girls know that Papa and I don't live together anymore. When our grocery shop closed, he left to join the Shan army. And I can't get a job to make money to feed us. Here you will be able to eat plenty of food every day," promises Mama. "I need to leave now for the long bus ride back to Shan State."

"No! No! No! I'm afraid. I love you so much. Please don't go!" I scream, tears running down my face.

"Wake up, Aye Sander. You're having another nightmare. It's okay. We're safe. Please wake up, sweet sister," says Thiri softly as she rubs my back.

Struggling to open my eyes, I see Thiri's concerned face staring down at me. Oh my. I'm relieved to know it was just a dream, but also disappointed that another dreadful nightmare occurred. They're infrequent these days, but still appear every once in a while.

It has been eight years since that day when Mama abandoned us here at the nunnery. I still feel as if it was yesterday. I was only five years old. Little sister Thiri was four. Mama took us on a long bus ride from Shan State to Yangon. Such a big, bustling, noisy city, crowded with bicycles, people pushing carts overflowing with bags of rice, buses packed full of people clutching chickens and packages. Thiri and I thought we were taking an adventure with Mama. That was what she had told us.

Disembarking from the bus, we walked for what seemed like forever. It was roasting hot and sticky with no cool breezes or fresh air like at home. We arrived at a large stone building. Many girls, big and small, wore pink robes and saris, their heads shaven. I had seen girls in these clothes at home. We called them Girls in Pink. I didn't know at the time that they were young nuns.

Holding each of our hands, Mama walked with us into the building where a woman greeted us and introduced herself as Daw Kumacari, the head nun. She showed us around the nunnery, inside and out.

"This big room filled with bunk beds is where you will sleep. Here's the kitchen. It's very large because we have many children and nuns to feed. This large room with small tables, chairs, and bookshelves serves as the classroom. And as you've noticed, there are many alters everywhere for our worshiping. Outside are the cooking fires. I'm sure this all feels overwhelming right now, but you will learn to know your way around here very quickly."

"Let's sit together and talk in this small bedroom." We follow Daw Kumacari into the room with Mama and sit on the bed. "This will be your new home, girls," Daw Kumacari says gently. Mama nods her head, as she looks down at the floor.

The next few moments replicate my reoccurring nightmare, ending with Mama kissing us on our foreheads and leaving forever. We have never seen Mama or Papa again. Never received a letter. Nothing at all. It was like they had died and gone to their next lives without saying goodbye.

After Mama left, Daw Kumacari introduced us to another nun who told us to take off all our clothes. She put a big towel around us and began to shave our heads. Thiri and I both loved our long beautiful curly blond hair. Suddenly, it was all around us on the floor, looking like a sea of snakes. We cried hysterically, even though the nun and Daw Kumacari told us to be brave and sit still.

Next thing we knew, the nuns were helping us to get dressed—a simple white tee shirt, a long pink sarong that fell from our waists to our ankles, tied with a cotton string, and a long piece of pink fabric that wrapped around our bodies like a sari and hung over our shoulders. We wondered what we looked like in these clothes, without any hair.

Daw Kumacari took us to the room where we would sleep. I was given a top bunk and Thiri was given the bed beneath me. There was a lightweight blanket and very thin pillow on each of our beds.

We were both tired, confused, and desperately sad. We asked Daw Kumacari if we could eat some food, as we hadn't eaten anything since leaving our home early that morning. She took us outside to the cooking fires where a giant pot filled with soup was loudly gurgling. She gave each of us a small cup filled to the top.

By that time, other girls in pink appeared, some older and some even younger than us. They started talking to us, but we couldn't understand their languages. As we ate our soup sitting outside on the rocks, we almost fell asleep.

Daw Kumacari noticed this. When we finished eating, she took us back to our beds. It was starting to get dark. When she left the room, I crawled down from the top bunk and cuddled up with Thiri. We quickly fell asleep—our first night in the nunnery.

Looking back over the past eight years of my life, I'm surprised how quickly time passed. Thiri and I adapted to our new daily routines. We woke each morning at 4 a.m. to the sound of the gong, hit over and over again quickly, then followed by a slow pace of pongs. The gong told us to wake up after our long night's sleep and start our day.

With 350 girls living in the nunnery, mornings were chaotic as we all dressed quickly in our pink robes, washed our faces, brushed our teeth, and filed into the eating room for rice porridge. Next were the morning chants, followed by school classes until 5 p.m. Private meditation time lasted until 9 p.m. We then joined together for prayers and were sent off to bed again.

Twice each month, we walked in a single file through the village with our alms bowls, asking for rice and donations. These walks gave us an opportunity to see how others in the village lived—simple thatched-roof homes, rag-tag children playing ball, dogs running in circles, bicycles maneuvering over dirt paths, and small shops selling foods. This village was bigger than our village in Shan State—more homes, people, dust, and noise.

Eleven teachers, mostly nuns, taught in our school. Sometimes a monk taught us a special session of the teachings of Buddha. We learned quickly that we must always show deference to monks by bowing, even to the most junior monk. And we absolutely must never offend or insult a monk, even if he insulted us.

In addition to Buddhist lessons, we learned to read, both in Burmese and English, and we learned arithmetic. Girls living at the nunnery came from many different ethnic states where languages other than Burmese were spoken. In our Shan State, Thiri and I learned Shan language. Having different languages made it difficult to talk to the other girls, so we didn't make friends with the others for a long time.

At first, we thought we would only live at the nunnery temporarily, until Mama found work. We asked Daw Kumacari when Mama was returning to take us home. She always said that she didn't know. We missed Mama every day. Days went by, weeks, months, and then years. Birthdays weren't celebrated. It was difficult to remember our ages.

As the years passed, I learned that most of us girls had been abandoned by parents. A few were orphans—their parents killed in war, or dead from hunger or disease. Our country was very poor, and parents struggled to earn enough money to buy food. When they saw their children weak from hunger, they took them to live in monasteries or nunneries, where they knew they would be fed and educated by the monks or nuns.

Even though I knew my story was not different from the others', I couldn't accept that I had been abandoned. At first, I felt like my heart had been stabbed and my body shattered into tiny pieces. It was difficult to breath and move. This pain lasted for months. When it finally subsided, I still felt sick to my stomach all the time. It was difficult to eat. The nuns told me I must keep up my strength by eating regularly.

I believed that I had deserved to be abandoned. I wasn't a good girl. I didn't deserve Mama and Papa. It was all my fault. I was ashamed of myself for causing them to give me away.

One day I noticed that I felt better physically. I had more energy. Then, I got angry. Why me?? Mama and Papa were evil and selfish!! Other girls in the world didn't suffer like this!! It wasn't fair!! Sometimes I was so angry I threw rocks at the building and shouted at the top of my lungs.

Sometime later, I laughed at another girl's joke. It felt good but strange. I couldn't remember the last time I had laughed.

I played chase the ball with Thiri. I felt proud of my test scores. I felt confident when talking to the nuns or the other girls. I started speaking up in class, asking and answering questions. I didn't have nightmares as frequently. I didn't know why I felt better, but I was happy about it.

When talking with Daw Kumacari one day, I told her all of this.

"Thank you for sharing this with me, Aye Sander. Actually, these are stages all girls and boys experience when they're abandoned. Your feelings, both physical and mental, aren't unique."

I found it a relief to know this. I had been starting to feel scared about my actions and wondering if I was crazy. But after learning about abandonment, I noticed more frequently when new girls looked sad or cried or yelled. I began reaching out to them, giving a hug, wiping their tears, whispering softly. I wanted to make them feel better. And I learned that helping them always made me feel good too.

I started paying more attention to Thiri and realized that she was always the one comforting me. She was like the big sister. She never acted out like me. She was just Thiri—easygoing, helpful, energetic. Maybe that was because she was only four when we arrived at the nunnery. She probably didn't remember as much about our village and happy times with Mama and Papa. Whatever the reason, I was happy to see that she seemed content.

Thiri had big dreams. She talked about becoming an engineer and traveling the world. Both of us were good students. We loved to read and were eager to learn more.

However, I had grown to love the monastic life. The meditation, classroom studies, friendships with girls and nuns were all soothing to me. Every day was the same. There were no surprises. I think I've always been happiest when in my head—thinking about life, Karma, finding peace.

I started to learn more about the work the nuns do. They cooked, taught classes, and cared for the girls. They taught Buddhist scripture, the Buddhist lifestyle. and meditation. They taught us to refrain from harm, to help others whenever we could, and to develop qualities like compassion and wisdom, benefiting all beings equally. Sometimes they helped other villagers who were sick or needed a place to sleep temporarily. I learned that nuns weren't rich in material goods, but were rich in love for all people.

I started thinking that maybe I could become a nun like Daw Kumacari. She and her sister Daw Hemacari decided at a young age to become nuns and open a school for vulnerable girls. Maybe Thiri and I could be like them—open a school for girls like us who had been abandoned.

Now thirteen years old, I'm just finishing secondary school level. Thiri still has one more year to go. Usually, girls leave the nunnery after completing their secondary grade classes. There just isn't enough room for the older girls because young girls continue to come to the nunnery every day.

If we want to stay longer, we need to become aspirants—girls who aspire to join the order. I need to have a serious talk with Thiri to find out if she might want to become an aspirant. I know I do. I hope she does also. I can't imagine what it would be like to live without Thiri by my side. She is like the other half of me—the half that is more calm and funny and protective. Without her, I'm nothing.

When we change into our nightgowns later that evening, I ask Thiri to sit by me so we can talk.

When I tell her that I've been thinking that maybe we could both become aspirants, she pauses then says, "Aye Sander, I've been wanting to talk with you about this. Even though I'm grateful for living here where it's safe, for being together with you, and for receiving a good education, I'm curious about the rest of the world out there. We don't even know much about our own country and people. We know our military junta fights with other armies in our country. We know many people are poor and hungry. We know the Buddhist teachings. But there must be so many things we don't know about at all."

Her words spill out. A confession. "You know I have always dreamt of traveling to see other countries and people. I have always wanted to be an engineer and build bridges and solve problems. I think you might love the monastic life more than me."

I must admit, I did know this, but I didn't really want to accept it. "I get scared when I think of leaving the nunnery," I confess. "And I'm not sure if I can live without you near to me. I think you are braver than me."

"But," I tell her, "I do want you to be happy. If you need to leave the nunnery for your happiness, I will understand. I will be sad, but I don't want you to give up your dreams."

Thiri, always so smart, suggests, "Before we make our big decisions, maybe we should talk to Daw Kumacari to ask questions and learn more about becoming an aspirant. What do you think?"

I agree, and in between classes the next day, I ask Daw Kumacari to sit with Thiri and me to learn more about becoming an aspirant.

"Being a nun in Burma is a bit different than in other countries," Daw Kumacari tells us. "Here, nuns aren't equal to monks in their rights. This is a Burmese law. This is why monks can accept alms every day of the year, but nuns can only accept them twice each month.

"Also, nuns in our country aren't fully ordained. There are novice nuns—girls in pink like you who live here and learn Buddhist teachings. If a girl wants to continue to live the monastic life, she first becomes an aspirant—one who desires to join the community, the Sangha. Traditionally, one stays in a Sangha for at least five years after committing to the monastic life.

"The purpose of the Sangha is to study and practice the Buddha's teachings, and, whenever possible, to share them with others. A monastic nun frequently serves as an 'honorary mother' to a young novice. When you officially join a Sangha, food, clothing, lodging, and medicine are provided to you.

"I think you have already learned many of the rules that must be followed by nuns, but let me remind you. We shave our heads and wear monastic robes, as symbols of our spiritual values. Shaving our heads symbolizes letting go of worldly concerns. We remain celibate—no husband or babies. We don't wear jewelry or makeup. We don't listen to or play music, except for chanting, of course. We don't dance or watch entertainment. And we are vegetarian. As we have a profound concern for all living beings, we don't want to contribute to the suffering of animals by eating them. And, as nuns, our emphasis is always on developing an internal focus."

Daw Kumacari, watches our faces then asks, "Does this make sense? Do you have questions? Or would you prefer to think on this for a while and talk with each other a bit? We can speak again tomorrow if you like."

I look to Thiri who says, "It's a lot all at once. And it requires big decisions for each of us, Aye Sander. Let's stop for now."

"That sounds smart," says Daw Kumacari with a smile.

Tucked into my bunk bed, I can't stop thinking about everything Daw Kumacari told us. It all sounds perfect to me. I know in my heart that I want to learn more of the Buddhist teachings and serve as a spiritual guide for other young girls or people in our village. I don't think I will miss the worldly things like makeup or music or dancing. And wearing a "uniform" rather than picking out clothes to wear each day sounds delightfully simple. Although I loved my long blond curly hair, my shaved head is much easier. My head does get a little cold at night sometimes, but I just put the blanket over my head, and then I'm fine. I wonder if Thiri is also breaking her brain, pondering all these decisions.

"Wake up, Aye Sander, the gong is sounding. Time to dress for breakfast and chants," Thiri says as she rubs my arm. "I've hardly slept at all. My mind was running laps all night, thinking about what we learned from Daw Kumacari yesterday. Thinking about what my heart wants me to do. Thinking about you. Let's find time to talk quietly with each other after our math class today."

I can hardly concentrate in class. All I can think about is what Thiri might say. I want to know, but I'm afraid to know. My rumbling nervous tummy worries it won't be good news for me.

"Let's sit outside on the big rocks," suggests Thiri after we complete class.

I follow her outside. It's a beautiful day—not too hot or humid or dusty or noisy. I can hear the melodic song of the sunbirds from their perches in the nearby trees. Maybe they're a good omen.

"Let's hold hands while we talk about this, Aye Sander," suggests Thiri as we settle down on the rocks. "You know how much I love you. We are each other's family and world. Even though my heart broke when Mama left us, I will always be thankful for the nuns and our life here in the nunnery. I think we're very lucky to have received an education here. Most girls in our country don't get to go to school.

"And I know how comfortable you are here. This is a big relief for me. You suffered so much pain, nightmares, and sadness when Mama left us. I think you have found a safe, enriching life here in this monastic community. I don't feel that I have to worry about you anymore.

"Over our years here, I've told you about my dreams. Dreams that entail me leaving the monastic life and entering the outside world. I still have those dreams."

"Oh, Thiri, you're going to leave me, aren't you??" I blurt with tears in my eyes.

"Wait, Aye Sander. I haven't finished yet," she responds. "I have a compromise to suggest."

"Daw Kumacari told us that aspirants usually stay in the Sangha for a minimum of five years. We're both still very young—you're only thirteen and I'm twelve. After five years, we'll both be teenagers."

"I'm thinking that we officially become aspirants, if accepted into the Sangha. After the five years, we can make a new decision again together. Possibly, I will want to stay in the monastic life. But maybe I will want to leave. I don't know today how I will feel then."

"But for now, I'm willing to stay with you. We're sisters always and forever, whether living together here in the Sangha or living apart. Our love will never disappear," Thiri whispers, hugging me tightly.

I cannot stop smiling. My face is covered with tears. "Oh, dear Thiri, I'm so happy. Thank you—thank you. You are too kind to me. I know you are making sacrifices for me." When I volunteer to tell Daw Kumacari our decision, it's with a smile so big it almost cracks my face in two.

After the day's classes end, the three of us sit together once again. Daw Kumacari is happy to hear we have decided to join the Sangha. When Thiri asks what happens next, she tells us that parents should provide approval for girls such as us who are younger than eighteen. "But," Daw Kumacari smiles, "since your parents aren't involved in your lives anymore, the Buddhist rules allow a respected nun in the Sangha to provide that approval. I am happy to do that for you."

"I've known you both for many years now, and have great respect for your kindness, attention to Buddhist practices, and morality.

"The next step is for the senior nuns to interview you. They'll ask many questions to learn your reasons and determinations. If they approve, you'll officially become aspirants and be assigned a spiritual guide. I would be most honored to serve as spiritual guide for both of you.

"But first, you need to 'take refuge' to confirm your commitment. This prayer conveys your commitment."

Looking each other in the eyes, we say the prayer together softly. We smile. We nod our heads.

We're becoming aspirants. We'll live the monastic life together—at least for five years.

To the excellent Buddha, Dharma,
and Sangha,
I go for refuge until enlightenment;
By the merit of giving and the rest,
May I attain buddhahood for the sake of all beings.

Chapter 3
Burma 2011 and 2015

Due to censorship within the country, lack of connection to the outside world, and restrictive travel rules, Burma was virtually closed off from the world for fifty years. People inside knew nothing of the world outside their immediate environment, not even their own country's ethnic states. Fear was the rule of order for the military junta. Any defiance was met with prison or death. No one made eye contact walking down the street. No one could be trusted.

However, in the first decade of the twenty-first century the military junta started easing restrictions for economic reasons. Wealth was their driving force. They realized they could not continue to prosper unless Burma assumed a more participatory role in the world.

People's hope for political change and democracy grew rapidly. Tourism began. Cell phones and the internet were activated. People learned about the outside world. The Burma I encountered at this time was a much different environment than the one I experienced during my first visit in 1974.

The beauty of the country and its people was transporting and familiar. I began following up on introductions and met with a group of young, committed social activists calling themselves EduNet. Ethnically and religiously diverse, their common goal was to help their people. These educated young men and women had joined together to maximize their capability to create change. Each had an area of expertise—music, art, library development, teaching. They fed off each other's passion and imaginations, all with an end goal of helping Burmese youth.

When speaking with one of these young women, I asked her what she would like to do to help her people if funding was available.

She told me there were no picture books for children. Books were definitely not a priority for the military junta. They had closed all the libraries and enacted strict publishing restrictions. Years ago, parents had borrowed books from street-side kiosks and were seen everywhere reading to their children. However, in the dark years of the military junta, parents didn't have time to read to their children. They were too busy struggling to earn money to feed them.

She told me of her dream to publish books of ethnic folktales for Burmese children. With 135 ethnicities in Burma, there were many folktales passed down by word of mouth. If she had funding to publish the books, she would find the folktales and "rewrite" them, creating her own copyright. Publishing would occur inside Burma, which would be less expensive and would avoid shipping inadequacies. Her country-wide connections to librarians and schools would facilitate distribution of the books. She had obviously formulated this plan in her head and was just waiting for someone to reach out to her.

With my determination to empower women and girls in Burma and her well-defined project plan in hand, I decided to move forward in creating a 501(c)(3) US-authorized nonprofit. Educational Empowerment (EE) became a reality in March 2012.

Living in the States and operating a nonprofit on the other side of the world required networks and connections. Where to start? I learned of a woman in my hometown community who also operated a nonprofit in Burma. A coincidence? Maybe not. I reached out to her for advice. She was more than happy to share lessons learned and to introduce me to some of her in-country Burmese partners. She was not territorial about her connections as are some in the nonprofit arena. I had a starting point.

Folktale picture books for children became EE's first output. We published forty different books in our folktale series, representing approximately twenty ethnicities. Some books were published in two languages, Burmese and English. Other folktales were published in three languages, adding in the ethnic dialect. Thousands of books were sent throughout the country each year. Children finally had picture books, and the folktales were preserved in print for future generations.

At that time, it was exciting to witness the rapid transition within Burma, as if the people had awoken from a deep slumber, refreshed and eager to move forward with plans. I rode the wave with them, opening my mind and heart to possibilities.

Additional project ideas for EE started surfacing. Education was our priority. We knew that only half of Burmese women completed primary education and that the quality of that education was often inadequate. Sadly, one in every four girls attending primary school was unable to read simple sentences about everyday life.

Primary barriers preventing girls' access to education were lack of schools, distance to schools, conflict, hunger, school fees, disabilities, and just being a girl. Even when access was available they were forced to balance their passion for education with family responsibilities.

When we heard that 2008's Cyclone Nargis had devastated 60 percent of the schools in the Delta region, building a new elementary school jumped to the top of our to-do list. In 2015, EE coordinated with another nonprofit, Helping the Burmese Delta, to select the location for the school. The village provided the site and the labor to construct the school. Although it was frequently difficult to engage Burma's school officials for accreditation, luck was on our side. We attained the necessary registrations and approval to obtain trained teachers for assignment to our school.

With news that school construction was completed, it was time to attend the official opening ceremony. The drive from Yangon to the jetty was five hours of long, straight two-lane roads through beautiful flat rural lands with rice paddies aplenty. Once at the jetty, we transferred to a small flat-bottom boat for another hour and a half, skimming through canals filled with hyacinth and views of ramshackle homes and active fisherman. Yangon and its crowded streets and traffic, left behind just that morning, was a world forgotten.

Before reaching our overnight destination, our guides decided to take a shortcut through a canal well known to them. Much to their surprise, the water was only knee deep. We ran aground in the mud several times, requiring the young (and fortunately strong) boatmen to punt and push until we were cleared. Being stuck in a canal in the dark in the middle of the Delta with no outside connectivity was unsettling. After a while, the inky black night became a backdrop for shimmering white twinkly lights that suddenly engulfed us—my first encounter with fireflies. Looking up at the heavens in wonder, I saw a bounty of stars looking down upon us.

We spent a restless night's sleep in a nearby village on the floor of their existing school. Waking to a beautiful sunrise, I was filled with anticipation to finally see our school in Htan Kyun village.

Approaching by boat, I heard music and saw canal banks lined with people. Disembarking, I was surrounded by throngs of children and parents as eager to greet me as I was to meet them. A corsage presented to me by a beautiful shy girl. Our beautiful school bedecked with balloons and streamers. So many smiling faces.

The village had never had a real school nor a real teacher. The village's old windowless school was a one-room shack that flooded each year during the rainy season. The village resident with the highest education used to serve as the teacher.Constructed on twelve-foot-high concrete feet, the new school was designed to survive the annual floods. Because of its height, it became the only structure sitting above water in the entire region during the rainy season. It was designated as an emergency hub for people needing water, medical supplies, and food during the floods. The rest of the year, the school provided essential education to the girls and boys in this forgotten land.

The villagers were proud to have constructed the school by themselves, and they were committed to maintaining it over the years to come. They truly owned it. It was a testament to their respect for the power of education and their belief that education would provide their children with endless opportunities.

In an area devastated by Cyclone Nargis, our sponsored school in this tiny village in the Delta was a gift to be remembered by all, including our numerous donors at home who had made it all possible.

Delta Waters

What's that screeching noise? Why are the walls creaking and shuddering? Why are birds squealing and goats mournfully bleating? I jump out of bed and run outside to see what's causing this horrendous havoc. Wind is madly whipping up the river and water is pouring over the banks.

Mama and Papa have already gone to the fields to work our crops. It's only me and my faithful friend Moe. The hairs on his back are standing alert and his nose snorts loudly. Neighbors run outside. We look at each other with fear-ridden faces. A coconut tree crashes to the ground. I feel that the world is falling apart before my eyes.

And then the rain pours from the heavens, drenching me. I can no longer see the river. The sky has become an evil dark red pit. I don't know what to do. I don't understand what is happening. My body is frozen.

Suddenly, I'm knee-deep in water. Moe is struggling to stay on his feet. The river is now pulling at my legs, and the wind tugs my hair and clothes. I hear a ghastly crash and see my neighbor's house float past me.

I wrap my arms around a coconut tree. The water keeps rising. Moe starts to float away. Thankfully his collar is reachable. I grab hold of it and pull him into my body, against the prickly coconut fronds. Rain fills my eyes. I wait and wait, hearing people and animals wailing.

Eventually, the light in the sky dims as darkness approaches. The water slowly recedes, leaving a sea of mud and debris, as if a giant angry monster has smashed our world to bits. Letting go of the tree, I can stand again, although my feet sink deep into the mud. I release Moe. The mud reaches his belly. It's difficult for him to move his four legs but he struggles on. I'm thankful that he's still alive.

Will this evil cyclone return or has it moved on to demolish other lands? I need to find Mama and Papa. My heart pounds with fear. Did they float away in the waters? I must search for them.

Suddenly, I open my eyes. I am still in my bed, Moe lying quietly beside me on the floor. The sun is shining and birds are singing. Taking a deep breath, I know that I dreamt of the cyclone again. It has been two years since it destroyed our Delta lands, killing 150,000 people, and orphaning 20,000 boys and girls. I am sixteen years old now, but I still dream of that day.

I hear Mama cooking in the kitchen. Thankfully, she and Papa survived the cyclone by clutching onto trees until it was safe to move. A rescue boat eventually came to our village on our small island in the Irrawaddy River. They told us of the dreadful devastation all around the Delta region. They brought us water and food supplies to help until we could fend for ourselves.

My best friend Kyaw survived, but both of his parents were killed. They were like family to me, and I still miss them terribly. Kyaw and I are the same age. He is like a brother to me. Mama and Papa took him in to live with our family. He was angry and sad at first but has finally started to smile again when I make silly jokes.

We are both very fortunate to have many aunties,

uncles, and cousins nearby. Some live on our island, and others live on the mainland across the river. We were all impacted by the cyclone. Working together now as a family to rebuild our homes, fishing boats, paddies, and gardens has been a blessing. We believe that having family nearby will help us to successfully rebuild our lives and to hopefully find new sources of income.

We're all of Karen ethnicity, as is much of the Delta region. That sense of community and identity has always been an important source of comfort and connection for me. Now, after the cyclone, it's even more significant—it helps me to feel safe again, optimistic about my future, and loved.

Music and dance is a particularly joyful part of our Karen culture. My uncle Win plays the Thana, a small seven-stringed harp. Auntie Hlaing plays the Gweh, made out of a buffalo horn, and cousin Cetan pounds the big drum. Together, they play songs symbolizing our folktale stories. When we young people are feeling energetic, we dance to the beat of the drum and sing along loudly.

If we aren't playing music together or doing chores together, we love to eat together, especially if it's fish. Fortunately, fish are readily available in the Delta. My favorite is a strong-tasting dish of fermented fish served over rice and vegetables with lots of hot chilies. I feel hungry just thinking about it.

I love Delta life. It's the only life I know. When I was born in 1994, Mama and Papa named me Maiah, one who is precious like an emerald. Mama wasn't able to carry any more babies, so I don't have any brothers or sisters like many of my friends. I am Mama and Papa's only gem.

Sitting at the foot of Burma, the Delta is remote. Almost all foods and supplies must be delivered by boat. Even though that's expensive, it's the only way to access our remote villages.

We experience flooding every year due to weather and tides, but it's beautiful during the dry season. I feel like I can walk forever, across the open, grassy fields with no one in sight. One of my favorite activities is watching the herds of ducks fluttering about in the salt water of the canal. They're herded just like sheep—even the incredibly big flocks. When it's time to leave the canal, Mrs. Duck Herder splashes them with water. They tend to be compliant followers, and quickly fall into line, meandering back to their nesting homes.

If there are no ducks to be seen, there's a bounty of multi-colored goats and swine. Water buffalo working hard in the fields or rolling in the mud. Chickens and roosters strutting with purpose. Baby crocodiles sunning on the banks.

We hear that some call the Delta the "rice bowl of Burma." Rice grows well in our climate and is a staple food for everyone in our country. I just hope that our ability to grow rice returns to its full strength, as it was before the cyclone.

For all the good things about life in the Delta, though, our people are very poor. My teachers in secondary school said we have one of the highest poverty rates in Burma. And the damage from the cyclone is making it even worse.

Two years after Cyclone Nargis hit our lands, we're starting to see changes. Some things are better than pre-cyclone days and some are worse.

Immediately after the devastation, the military junta blocked support from large international relief groups. Visas for aid workers were delayed. Foreign helicopters and boats that might have made life-saving deliveries were turned away. Aid agencies were denied access to our lands. Journalists were not allowed to report from our disaster area.

Regular folk felt that the military junta put their hatred of the international world ahead of the well-being of their own people. They didn't prioritize our lives.

In response to their lack of support, civil society groups and individuals from all areas of our country stepped up to help. They raised money, collected supplies, and traveled to badly affected parts of the Delta to help survivors in their shattered villages. As these recovery efforts gained momentum, more and more community-based organizations and civil society groups organized themselves, gaining unprecedented experience in providing humanitarian relief.

Kyaw and I have been observing these people, admiring what they do and how they do it. Both of us completed secondary schooling in our village. We both assumed we would attend high school somewhere in the Delta and possibly attend college in Yangon, but after the cyclone we aren't sure whether there's a single high school left standing in the entire region.

We hear from aid workers that most Delta women, whether married or not, lost their source of income after the cyclone. They tell us that new "cash-for-work" programs are now available—an option to earn money while restoring destroyed roads, bridges, and jetties. Women involved in these programs are included in the decision-making processes, increasing the likelihood of their future involvement in other construction activities.

More women are starting small businesses—grocery stores, clothing making/tailoring shops, fish brokering services, free funeral services. Some are making and selling our special Karen clothing for people who lost all of their belongings in the cyclone. The Karen's unique embroidered designs and colors help us to easily recognize our people.

Women are finally being included in leadership roles, especially as youth migrate out of the Delta in search of job opportunities up north.

The aid workers tell us that rebuilding schools and restoring education systems after a disaster are especially crucial to helping girls regain a sense of normalcy and security. We are always easy targets for assaults. Being in school and learning about our rights gives us internal strength. It reminds us that we don't have to be victims—we can be warriors.

Post-cyclone, the Delta continues to suffer from lack of basic shelter for people, lack of schools, broken road and bridge infrastructures, lack of access to clean water, and lack of health care. Although cellular phone service is slowly becoming available in Yangon, there is no phone service in the Delta yet.

In Karen culture, smoking or chewing tobacco and drinking whiskey is part of our fireside routines and celebrations. And the smoking also helps to keep insects at bay. However, I have seen an increase in this substance use since the cyclone. Although it's probably a reflection of the elders' stress while trying to rebuild our lives, I hope it doesn't become a forever habit.

We learn from the aid workers that the most important factors affecting a family's ability to recover quickly after a disaster are tangible assets such as land, local job opportunities, income, ability to manage household resources, aid, and the health and number of working family members.

Between Kyaw's extended family and mine, we believe we're fairly well positioned for recovery: together, we own more than two hectors of land; we plan to seek out non-agricultural jobs to supplement our farming incomes; our elders are effective household managers; and we have many able-bodied youths and adults in our families, ready to work.

We're actively trying to rebuild our lives. We've made new paddy fields and gardens. Papa and my uncles have started fishing again. New chickens and ducks have arrived. Smells of cooking have returned. But this reconstruction is slow, hampered by lack of electricity and fresh water and the difficulty of accessing our island.

Besides Kyaw, other village children orphaned by the cyclone are also being taken in by families in our village. My uncle and auntie took in two little boys who lost their parents and still can't talk about the horrors of that day.

Kyaw and I want to help with the rebuilding. Although we've been working in the paddy fields and helping to build homes destroyed by the cyclone, we're only sixteen, with our whole lives ahead of us. Seeing what the aid workers do, we think we should be able to accomplish more than what's possible on our tiny island.

We know that education could help us to expand our skills and potentials. We need to find a high school. We need to learn more. We need to prepare to be leaders and advocates for our Karen people.

I find Kyaw sitting by the water, taking a break from planting rice in our new paddy field. "Kyaw, let's talk about finding a high school to attend." I begin. "I heard rumors that there's a high school down south in Yay Kyaw Toe village that survived the cyclone. It's being run by an international organization. It provides boarding for the students. Acceptance into the program is very competitive. It's hard work—long days in classes, long nights studying. All to achieve high scores on the annual exams. But is sounds perfect for us. We could learn critical thinking and master our English. It would be much better than high school programs we have seen around here."

Kyaw gets excited as I describe the school. "Wow, Maiah, that sounds fantastic," he exclaims. "I want to try out for it. I hope we can both be accepted. It would make it much easier if we're together. We can help each other to stay strong and motivated. How do we apply?"

"Each of us needs to write a letter to the school, telling about ourselves, our reasons for wanting to attend, and how a high school diploma would help us.

"That part could be hard," I say. "I know that I want to learn more about how I can help my people. But I don't exactly know what that looks like. Do I want to be a doctor or nurse? Or maybe a teacher? Or maybe a disaster aid worker? I do know that speaking English and understanding how to identify and solve problems are skills that can be applied to many jobs. I hope that the high school will help me decide which job I most want."

"I've always dreamt of becoming an engineer," says Kyaw thoughtfully. "I'm sure that requires special college courses and degrees, but high school is the first step. The new school year starts in two months. We better hurry to submit our letters. I hope we're not too late!"

He is right to worry. It might take a couple of weeks for our letters to reach the school. All our mail goes by boat, and there's still a lot of disruption and unpredictability of mail delivery. "Let's write our letters tonight after we finish our chores," I say excitedly, "and keep your fingers crossed for good luck!"

The next morning, Kyaw and I nervously hand our application letters to the driver of the mail boat. We both stayed up late into the night, thinking and writing our letters by candlelight. It was more difficult than I'd imagined to clearly express my dreams. But I did my best. Now the waiting begins.

It will be horrible if only one of us is accepted into the school. If Kyaw is accepted and I'm not, I'll be thrilled for him. But I will also be devastated for me. I will question "what's wrong with me? didn't I express my reasons well? are my dreams not important? is it because I'm a girl?"

I know that education for girls in our country isn't considered as important as education for boys. I've never understood that. We're just as smart, if not more. We're also strong and clever. And I think we're better at getting along with others and working as a team. It's definitely not fair.

Worrying about the school's decisions will not make the time go faster and will not change the outcomes. I'll keep my ears open for any other high school options in case I'm not accepted. And I have many chores to do, which will keep me busy. I've done all I can do for now.

Kyaw and I hug each other tightly and walk off together to work in the paddy fields.

Two Years Later

With pride in our hearts, tears in our eyes, and smiles cracking our faces, Kyaw and I join the students lining up to receive our high school diplomas.

We did it! We were both accepted into the Yay Kyaw Toe high school. We struggled through the two years of hard work and long nights. At times, we worried that we would fail, but we didn't. We prevailed!

There are twenty of us girls and boys who successfully completed high school. We come from all areas of the Delta. Some suffered more than others from the cyclone, losing their entire families to the raging water in a moment.

What we all share is our belief in the importance

of education to create change—in our lives, our family's lives, and throughout the entire Delta region.

We learned to speak English. We learned the importance of keeping our bodies strong, as well as our minds. We learned to treat others with kindness and understanding. We learned how to solve problems, whether developing clean water sources, acquiring electricity, effectively working with large groups, or improving basic infrastructures.

The line of graduates moves forward slowly, as the headmaster shares a little about each student before handing over their diploma. Mama and Papa sit in the front row, waiting patiently for our turns at the podium. Sunshine reflects off the gold of the nearby pagoda. Cows in adjacent fields moo quietly. A sense of peace hangs over us, as if time has stopped to acknowledge the significance of this moment.

Kyaw is in front of me in line. His turn is next. The headmaster tells everyone how fast Kyaw learned his lessons, how he helped tutor other students, and how he displayed a unique ability, through listening and asking questions, to motivate others to continue trying until they succeed. As Kyaw accepts his diploma, Mama and Papa stand, clapping their hands and cheering loudly.

Now it's my turn. I shake hands with the headmaster as he tells the audience of my perseverance, my creativity, and my demonstrated leadership traits of empathy and motivation. He also says that my skills will make me an outstanding teacher.

Mama and Papa are still standing and cheering.

My eyes are overflowing with tears as I proudly accept my diploma.

All of us students gather together, hugging and congratulating each other. After two years of living and studying together, we feel like a family. I hope we stay connected to each other over the coming years.

When I applied to this high school, I didn't know what I wanted to do with my life. I learned through school that I enjoy helping others with their lessons. As the headmaster stated, I seem to have the traits to make a good teacher.

I've heard that international organizations are working in villages to build new schools throughout the Delta. Unlike our prior schools, which were not built to withstand the rains and flooding of the Delta, the new schools are built off the ground on twelve-foot-high cement blocks. They have actual windows, doors, and roofs. Some even have toilets, safe from the rising waters. And the improved building construction keeps books and supplies dry.

To be an authentic teacher, the government requires certification. I have decided to become certified and find a job at one of these new schools.

My mantra for all the girls I meet will be "Believe in yourself. Don't be afraid to fail. Try anything you want. Even if you fail and make mistakes, try again. You might be successful next time."

Even though Kyaw always wanted to be an engineer, he has now decided to become an aid worker, like the people we met after the cyclone. He knows he is good at organizing others. And he wants to help people in need, as he received help. He plans to immediately reach out to some of the organizations we met to ask them about job positions. I can tell he is excited about his decision.

When I meet Kyaw on the other side of the graduation stage, I have tears in my eyes. "Well, my brother, we accomplished a great deal here at school." I tell him. "Thank you for sharing this experience with me. Without you, I don't know whether I could have made it. I love you and am very proud of you."

"You will always be my sister, Maiah. Love you back! Let's find Mama and Papa and eat some of the tasty Karen food out on the tables."

CHAPTER 4
Burma 2016

When global leaders met in 2016 for the United Nations General Assembly to establish new goals, the face of their agenda was the adolescent girl—a girl in school, safe, not married off, and able to follow her dreams. Global communities were called upon to commit critical investments in quality education, skills, training, access to technology, and other learning initiatives to prepare girls for life jobs and leadership.

Nations were also called upon to develop safety mechanisms for girls. One-third of women and girls in the world are beaten, forced into sex, or abused. One in five are a victim of rape or attempted rape. In conflict zones, such as Burma, gender-based violence runs rampant. Education is one answer, changing the mindset of girls and women that they deserve equal rights and safety.

At this same time, Pakistani education activist Malala Yousafzai released her powerful book about her struggle for education as a girl. It seemed to be the perfect message for adolescent-age girls in Burma.

My mantra of "it never hurts to ask" kicked in—I reached out to Malala's publisher for permission to translate I Am Malala into Burmese. Once again, my mantra proved true. Contracts were signed. A Burmese translator was enlisted. A mechanism to publish and distribute the books to adolescent girls across Burma was developed. And thousands of Burmese girls read Malala's inspiring book extolling the power of education to change their lives.

Resilience

It's almost time to open the doors. "Help me, Tun and Seng. These empty boxes need to go outside. I don't want children tripping over them."

Looking around the room, I'm tickled by the cheerfulness of wall colors, checkered floor mats, bright pink stools, a bounty of books, posters celebrating reading, natural light, and fresh air. The kaleidoscope of colors vibrates with invitation.

Peeking outside, I see mamas, boys, girls, grandmas—big smiles of anticipation on their faces, patiently waiting for me to open the doors to Myitkyina's new library. I've waited a long time for this moment—working hard, imagining how I would feel, praying that all would go well. Sometimes I knew I could do this; other times, I thought not.

But here I am—proud of myself and excited to share a love of reading with these sweet boys and girls.

"Okay Tun and Seng, are we ready??"

"Yes, Mama," they giggle. "Let's open the doors and start the fun."

Outside, I see curiosity on the children's faces and confusion on the parents' faces. I'm not surprised. Our people don't know why one would visit a library nor what to do there. I learned several years ago that starting a library isn't about hanging up a sign and opening the doors. It's about orienting the community to the benefits of a library and enticing them into this glorious new world.

"Welcome everyone," I say, stepping back to

make way. "Please come in and see all the pretty books. Make yourself comfortable on the stools or the mats. We'll be starting games and contests soon. There's tea and treats outside in the back. If you find books you want to take home to read, we'll let you borrow them for a week or two. Let me know when you have questions."

Libraries are just now coming alive again in our country. Over the past fifty years of dictatorship, libraries ceased to exist. They weren't a priority for the military junta.

My children's library is the first in Myitkyina, Kachin State. It will provide English and Burmese books, facilitate early literacy, and encourage a love of reading and investigation for the children.

I know that books will expand their minds, build confidence, and improve their thinking skills. Through games and storytelling, I'll teach the children that books are fun and an exciting source of knowledge. This space will open their minds to creativity and their dreams will grow big.

A friend told me that libraries in America are a matter of course. People know they're places to borrow books versus buying them. They know they can conduct research for a school project or attend fascinating lectures on travel, crafts, or whatever piques their fancy. They know they'll find a comfy nook to tuck into and lose themselves in an exciting picture book. And they know it's a glorious refuge for solitude, musty book smells, and delightful worlds to be explored.

People here have to learn all that. I want my library to teach them.

Back in the 1950s libraries actually existed in Burma. Women were trained to develop libraries and to obtain and categorize books. I had heard that some old library buildings in Burma's bigger cities were being reclaimed and I sought out some of these older trained librarians.. They understood how libraries create a safe haven for children, and how transporting a book's storyline can be for children and they readily agreed to pass on what they knew about library start-up development. They taught me the Dewey Decimal System, how to train budding new librarians in operational processes, and how to create an inviting environment to be explored. I'll always be thankful for their patient teachings and time.

My husband Zaw Kan helped me to build the library—construction, painting walls, installing doors and windows, picking up book orders. And my beloved children, Tun, now a big boy of six, and his four-year old sister Seng, provided a child's perspective—helpful when selecting books, arranging the room, and drawings posters for the walls.

Thinking back to my childhood, I'm still surprised at what I've accomplished and the resilience residing inside me. I was one of five children, with an absent father and a mother driven to beat us. When I was twelve years old, I was sexually abused by my neighbor—a teenage boy. I now understand how these abuses seriously impacted my self-confidence.

It wasn't until later in life that I learned of the prevalence of domestic violence in Burma. Under Burma's law, marital rape isn't a crime unless the wife is younger than fourteen years old. There aren't any women's shelters as safe havens for victims of domestic violence. The most common coping strategy for women in dealing with abuse is to stay silent.

Our Karen community down south in the Delta is one of the poorest regions in the country. My brother, sisters, and I learned quickly to eat when food was available, keep our lips zipped when Mama was in a mood, and do our chores when told. Our small village had one primary grade school. It flooded every year. Our teacher was whichever villager had completed the highest level of schooling. Sometimes that was only third grade.

I hunkered down and tried to remain invisible. I don't remember having big dreams or any dreams at all. When I was fifteen, my sister Lwin and I left home, caught a bus to Yangon, and found a monastery to sleep in for a few weeks. The monks helped us find work in a tea shop and let us attend classes at the monastery. Eager to learn, I gradually picked up Burmese, a little English, and mathematics.

I remember being so excited the first time I entered the monastery's library, I didn't want to leave. At that time, I could only read a few of the books. But I became determined to eventually read them all. The books opened my mind and my heart. I started feeling optimistic about a future filled with love, self-confidence, children, and a purpose. I became determined to rise above my childhood and to prevail, no matter what. I knew that a good education would be my liberator.

That's when I met Zaw Kan. He and I joined a

group of young people eager to help other youths in our country. Zaw's interest was music. He believed that music created solace our country desperately needed. Having personally experienced the benefit of books and libraries, my interest was library development. Others in our group focused on art, team building, or psychosocial training. Our passion and energy propelled us through many projects we were able to implement in monasteries and nunneries throughout Yangon's poor outskirts.

When celebrating my nineteenth birthday, Zaw proposed to me. Even though he was of Kachin ethnicity and I was Karen, we were both Christian, which eliminated some potential obstacles. I accepted and we moved to Myitkyina to live with his family until we could afford our own home.

Now, seven years later, we still live with his family, after numerous add-ons to the house. Tun and Seng fill our hearts with joy every day. And the dream of my own library is now a reality.

Like many women who juggle multiple responsibilities, I sometimes worry that I'm not a good mother or good leader or a good wife. I try to be a positive role model for girls and boys. I teach Tun to treat girls with respect and to value their contributions in the world. I teach Seng to think big with her dreams, to be strong, and to trust her instincts. And I remind myself every day how lucky I am to have this life.

And then, the day after the library's grand opening, my life falls apart.

"Pawlin, I need to speak with you," says Zaw quietly.

We wait until after dinner, when Tun and Seng have gone to bed, then sit together outside watching the sun sink behind the mountains.

"This is difficult for me to say, so I'm just going to spit it out," says Zaw. "Recently, I ran into my former high school sweetheart Jin. I think I've spoken of her a few times."

"That's wonderful, Zaw. How is she doing?"

"She's well. She never married. She tells me it's because she never met anyone who could compare to me."

"Oh," I stutter.

"Well, it's like this. We've seen each other quite a few times now. I want to be honest with you. My old feelings for her have returned, slamming me hard in my heart. I want to be with her permanently."

I can't breathe. I can't cry. I can only say, "But we're married. We have two young children."

"Yes, that makes it complicated. I think we should get a divorce," Zaw says hopefully.

"You must be joking," I say.

He knows divorce negatively impacts a woman's life in our culture. No matter the circumstances, everyone assumes it's the wife's fault. Divorce creates a shroud over the woman for the rest of her life, even if she remarries. She is still a divorcee.

"I don't want to divorce you!" I exclaim.

He has no pity. "The only other alternative is for you to leave here. This is my family's home and my Kachin community. Maybe you and the children should move back to Yangon."

"I can't talk about this anymore right now, Zaw. You are breaking my heart. Tun's and Seng's hearts will also be shattered." I'm angry and disappointed in him for being so selfish. I thought he was different from other men. I was wrong. Sobbing, I run into the house to smother my tears in our bed, fearful of waking the children.

Waking up the next morning, I forget for a moment about Zaw's plans, but the horror of it all quickly returns in full force. What should I do? What about my library that I worked so hard to create? How will I tell Tun and Seng that their Papa doesn't want to live with us anymore? They love their Papa and will probably think it's somehow their fault.

If I do move back to Yangon, I'll need to immediately find work and somewhere to live. I guess I shouldn't depend on Zaw to help us financially, as he is obviously so selfish.

I remind myself that I've always been resourceful. As a little girl with many siblings and worthless parents, being quick-witted and inventive was essential to my survival. Lately, I'd assumed that my life here in Myitkyina was the final chapter of my life's book, one that would continue on without much disruption, pain, or change. I guess I've been complacent and naive. Once again, I need to pull on my strength and use my creative brain to figure out how to move forward.

Our pastor recently told our congregation that life holds many paths from which to choose. Even though changing to a new path can be scary because of the unknowns, it might lead to surprising and wonderful outcomes. Maybe I'll discover a new life path where I can still be happy.

Keeping Seng and Tun safe, happy, and loved is my most important priority. As a good mama, I'll need to ensure that whichever path I take next will work for them also.

Maybe I should call my friend Su who works for an international nonprofit in Yangon called Helping Girls. She might have some job ideas, especially at the Helping Girls organization. I remember her telling me that they support adolescent girls all around the country. Many of the girls have suffered abuse, as have I.

Ouch. I already have a headache. I need to wake up, put on my happy face, and feed Tun and Seng. I wonder if Zaw is around. I will hold my tongue in front of the children, but what I really want to do is hit him over the head with a frying pan and rant and rave.

Walking into the kitchen, I see Zaw drinking a cup of tea and filling Tun's and Seng's bowls with rice porridge.

"Mama, good morning," Seng says with a happy smile. "You don't look good. Are you sick?"

"I'm fine, sweet girl. I just didn't sleep well last night. When you and Tun finish your porridge, please go outside to play for a bit. I want to speak with Papa."

As they run outside, I turn to Zaw. "I will pack our belongings and leave Myitkyina as soon as I find a temporary home in Yangon. I will need some money from you—maybe 10,000 kyat each month. Tun and Seng are your children. It's your responsibility as their papa to care for them. You will be the one to tell them that we're leaving. That isn't my responsibility. They'll be confused and sad. I do not plan to divorce you at this time or maybe ever. You will not sleep in our bed while I am still here. Do you agree to all of this?"

Silently, Zaw nods his head. I can't stand to look into his face, so I turn around and walk out of the kitchen.

Outside, I sit with the sun warming my face and my mind racing. I need to call Su. I'm so thankful that our country finally has cell phones. Before the military junta let us have this connectivity, our only options were to use rare landline phones or write letters—and postal service was slow and erratic. Now, everyone seems to have a cell phone glued to their ear.

"Su, it's Pawlin. Do you have a few minutes to talk to me?"

"Of course, Pawlin. Good to hear from you. Everything okay?"

"You won't believe my news," I say slowly and tell her the whole story, including the part about needing to move and looking for a job at Helping Girls.

"I can't believe what you're telling me, my friend!" exclaims Su. "I thought Zaw Kan was one of the good guys out there. I guess he's just like so many other men—selfish and not to be trusted. I'll check with my boss and let you know soon. Will call you back this evening. Be strong, if you can."

"Thanks, Su. My heart is destroyed. I appreciate your help."

Time seems to stand still as I wait for Su's call. I try to keep up a normal routine for Tun and Seng. Zaw plans to tell them tonight about our move, after he returns home from work. I assume he'll make up some story about our reason for moving being a need for more money. He promises to close up the library for me. I'll never have the chance to see children and parents enjoy my creation. Can't think about that right now. Too sad.

As soon as I hear my phone ring, I grab it. "Su, any good news for me??"

The news is excellent. A counselor position, working with girls who have suffered abuse.

"I know you have personal experience with this," says Su. "My boss believes you'll be an inspirational role model for these girls."

Tears spill from my eyes. My friend has saved me. I vow to her, "helping these girls will help me too. I'll share my story with them. I'll tell them 'You are NOT weak. You are strong. Do NOT let others look down on you. Do NOT tolerate any form of abuse or harassment.' I know I will be able to help them and teach them to never compromise their dreams."

"Su," I ask, "Seng, Tun, and I will catch the bus to Yangon tomorrow. Can we stay with you for a few days until I find us our new home?"

"Of course. It will be a tight squeeze, but we're all used to that anyway, aren't we?"

I thank her from the bottom of my heart.

With my mind lightened a bit from Su's news, I find the children. I need their hugs. Tomorrow will be a busy day. I know Seng and Tun will be confused about this sudden rush, move, and Papa's news. I'll try to make it sound like an exciting adventure. Hopefully, I will successfully keep my composure and pull it off.

Surprisingly, I'm feeling optimistic about this new job. I used to keep my childhood abuse a secret. I was embarrassed about it. I never even told Zaw Kan. In retrospect, I know my outlook could have changed if I'd only had someone to talk to. Now, I can be that someone for these girls. That feels good. I wonder if this has always been my destiny.

Even though I wish none of this old-girlfriend disaster was happening, I feel confident, knowing I can still be resourceful, resilient, and depend on myself. I'll open my heart to possibilities and see where this new path takes me.

Chapter 5
Burma 2017

Educational Empowerment's mission was purposefully broad enough to encompass multiple approaches to empowerment through education. With guidance from one of EE's treasured Burmese partners, we implemented a microfinance project for women in a small village near Bago. A $30 loan enabled a woman to start a small business—bicycle repair, selling fish soup, marketing grocery products. Women earned household income, and attained increased decision-making power, self-confidence, and community influence.

The bonus benefit was that the additional income enabled their daughters to stay in school rather than dropping out to earn money for the family.

Women helping women became the village mantra. I was especially touched to learn that I was the first American woman the loan recipients had ever met. My heart warmed to be a part of their strength and newfound self-reliance.

Watching the women stand tall with pride and independence, I found my voice at last. I was no longer a passive observer. I was a participant and an advocate. Unlike my stilted interactions with CPI's project recipients, relationships with my Burmese partners and recipients were authentic and heart-felt. These connections gave me as much, if not more, than EE and I gave to them.

Standing Tall

It happened so suddenly. Even though I knew his death was coming, I'm still surprised. Yesterday, he was here, wrapped in his bedding near the fire, and now he is gone. Passed away while I slept. My eyes are dry. Maybe the tears will come later when reality settles in.

Khin's soft breathing warms my heart. These precious peaceful morning moments are always a blessing. When she rouses and realizes her Papa has passed, shock and heartbreak will erupt.

So much to do now to prepare for Aung's funeral and cremation. We should have planned earlier, when we learned his liver disease was fatal, but he hadn't been able to face the reality of his pending death. I knew to not push him on anything, especially that. He'd been like a landmine waiting to detonate.

He hadn't always been like that. Memories of our first meeting fourteen years ago still make me smile. I was sixteen years old, living with my mama and older brother Thant. Papa had already moved abroad to Malaysia to earn money for our family. Aung had recently moved to our village to live with his uncle in hopes of learning a trade on the local farms.

It hadn't taken long for word to spread that a good-looking teenage boy had moved into our village. Most of the teenagers in the village had known each other since birth. A new boy was a curiosity, at the least.

While collecting water one sunny afternoon, we met for the first time at the spring. Being a shy, quiet young woman, I wasn't sure what to say.

"Hello," I stammered. "My name is Daw Ni. Are you the new boy in our village?"

"Yes, I am Aung. I come from Shan State where the endless tall mountains and green valleys make my heart sing. But there's little work. I hope to find a job here. Do you work?"

"A little part-time work in the fields. I had to stop school after primary grades. Mama and Papa needed me to help at home and bring in some money."

"Me too," chimed in Aung. "I had to work and didn't get to attend secondary school. You sure are pretty, Daw Ni."

I could feel my face blushing with red hot heat. No one has ever called me pretty, except Mama.

"Do you want to meet here again next week, Daw Ni?"

"Okay, that sounds like fun," I said with a smile, my heart beating loudly.

All through the week, I couldn't stop thinking about Aung—so good looking, tall and lanky, big dimples when he smiled. I second guessed everything I had said, assuming I must have sounded silly. When the time came to meet again, my head struggled with thoughts—what to wear, what to talk about, would he still think me pretty.

Owning only hand-me-down longyi skirts, tee shirts, and flip flops, there wasn't much to choose from to wear. My long black hair, usually pulled back into a bun, was more a nuisance to me than a possible attraction. I'd always assumed I was ugly as a rat, which my brother Thant told me many times. Tall for my age, I felt like a big lumbering giant.

Arriving at the spring the next morning, Aung was already there, playing at bouncing little rocks off the water. "Wow. You're good at that," I said, gathering a handful of rocks to try my own luck.

"I had a lot of practice at home—many streams to choose from. Want to have a contest?"

I agreed, knowing that he would probably win. I didn't really care. I was more interested in spending time with him.

We met every Saturday for several weeks—joking, making fun of each other, flirting. There was an obvious undercurrent of attraction between us. Eventually, I invited him for dinner to meet Mama.

"He seems like a very nice young man, Daw Ni. Just make sure he treats you well. Many men turn their life frustrations onto their wives—beating them, degrading them. You deserve love and kindness," warned Mama.

"I will try my best," I promised.

Our friendship and courting continued. We married two years later, and our sweet girl, Khin, was born the year after. We were still so very young, and suddenly we were parents.

Thant had decided to follow Papa to Malaysia, looking for work. So, it was just Mama, Aung, me, and Khin living together in our one room home. Fortunately, the plot of land and house had been in our family for generations, so we had a place to live.

Aung eventually found work at a local rubber tree farm. Although it didn't pay much, it was steady work. I found part-time work husking corn and picking fruit at several of the nearby farms. Mama cared for Khin while we worked.

These times were not easy, but they were pleasant. Our village, Kamarnut, changed little. It's a short bus ride outside Bago, a prominent rice- and timber-producing city. Yet Kamarnut is a simple, poor village. Small, dusty dirt streets and pathways connecting the 1,000 households. Thatched-roof homes raised off the ground providing shade cover during the hot season, space for animals, and small garden plots. Oxen and carts plentiful for farming. No indoor plumbing. Streams overflowing during the rainy season, requiring transport by row boat or sloshing through mud. No glass windows—only shutters to pull closed during monsoon season. Everyone knowing each other's business.

Sufficient food was always our primary concern. Aung and I continued to laugh and enjoy each other. Khin brought happiness and smiles to our faces each day with her silly antics and sweet disposition.

Thankfully, we were all healthy. There was no severe flooding nor fighting between the military junta and ethnic forces. Our country was still closed to the world, thanks to the military junta, but we didn't miss what we had never known.

Other than Khin and Mama, my biggest blessing in life was my friendships with village women I'd known since birth. We knew each other's secrets and dreams. Sitting together on our porches in the late afternoons drinking tea, we laughed at life and cried out our sorrows. These bonds were a saving grace during hard times.

One of my best friends, Ma Thet, suffered many twists and turns throughout her life. A widow of four years, she constantly struggled to earn enough money to feed her three children. Her dream was to open her own cigar business. She was intrigued with the meditative process—sitting cross-legged on the mat, sprinkling tobacco leaves, stems, and roots onto the small thanatphet leaves, peppering it with wood chips, and tightly rolling up the little cheroots. Smoking these cheroots was a big part of life for both men and women in our village. Ma Thet firmly believed a cheroot business could be a big money-maker if she was ever able to start her own shop.

My other close friend, Mu Mu, expanded her household a couple of years ago when she and her husband adopted her young niece. Sadly, Mu Mu's sister had disappeared while on a trip to Malaysia. Mu Mu's family became a household of four. Mu Mu has always been the one interested in looking pretty, experimenting with her makeup and hair styles. My oh my, so many memories of endless giggles erupting from our bellies when she showed up with bright blue eye makeup and pigtails scattered all over her head.

One day Mu Mu and Ma Thet asked me about my dreams. "Daw Ni, what would you want to do if anything was possible? Who would you want to be? Tell us your dreams!"

"I don't think I have dreams like that. It's impossible for me to imagine a life outside our village. I love our village, and don't want to leave it," I said thoughtfully. "I do love to cook, and I've been told that my sticky rice is the best ever. But that doesn't seem like a very big ambition. This is the life I know. This was Mama's life and my grandma's life.

They complained at times. But they never thought there was a different option. As they would say, we are only women. We were not seen as having skills, brains, or the ability to provide for our families without a man."

"That's gloomy, Daw Ni," Mu Mu said with a sad face. "I think that women are smarter than men usually. We intuitively know what to say and how to treat people. We're not afraid to show our emotions. We just haven't been given a chance to shine and show our intelligence and creativity."

"You are totally right, Mu Mu," Ma Thet said enthusiastically.

"I'll try to think bigger," I agreed. However, I didn't give it much thought. There was always just day-to-day life in my focus.

When Papa had left for Malaysia, Mama had taken over management of our household money and decisions. There was no one else to do it. Unfortunately, she never received much respect from the men of the village. Such was a woman's fate. Being Buddhist, we were conditioned to believe that men are inherently superior. Our Karma determined our wealth, power, talent, and gender in the next life. Many Buddhist men prayed they wouldn't be re-born as a female. Heaven forbid—being a woman meant a life of subservience.

"Daw Ni," I chastised myself. "enough of this dwelling on the past. There is much to be done today."

As decreed by Buddhist tradition, Aung's body will be viewed for seven days and then cremated. I need to notify the monks and seek their assistance with the funeral. News will spread quickly throughout our village.

The meager savings we accumulated over the early years of our marriage have evaporated. When dear sweet Mama passed, our savings were used for her funeral. Aung's ability to work ended shortly thereafter. His liver disease sapped his strength and he wasn't able to contribute income to our family. Truthfully, he lost his will to live.

Papa stopped sending money home years ago. Mama and I didn't hear a peep from Thant after he moved to Malaysia. There won't be any support available to me from my family.

Thankfully, as traditional in Buddhism, money will be gifted to us to show sympathy. This pek kim will offset funeral costs during our grieving time.I have absolutely no idea what will become of Khin and me. I'll try not to worry about that today though. First, I need to get used to the fact that I am now a widow.

Luckily, widowhood in Buddhism is not looked down upon as it is in some religions. We don't have to advertise our widowhood by shaving our heads or abandoning our jewelry. We aren't forced to fast or sleep on hard floors to demonstrate our humiliation about widowhood. We don't have to stop attending life celebrations. Most importantly, we can remarry if we choose to do so.

Would I want to remarry? If I married again, would my new husband be able to earn income for me and Khin? Would he be willing to help care for Khin? Would he help with chores? Would he respect me and treat me with dignity?

Ma Thet hasn't remarried since her husband died. We were just speaking about her widowhood the other day.

"Ma Thet, have you ever wanted to marry again?" I asked.

"Well, I might consider it if I met the right man. As far as men in our village, I certainly haven't seen any attractive single men lately. They appear to be in short supply."

She told me about other widows she knew and their struggles, being the only caregiver in the home. "I've heard that starvation among widows is widespread throughout our country. Some simply can't take care of their children and earn income at the same time. Also, we're extremely vulnerable to sexual abuse. Even more tragic, I've heard of widows selling their daughters to trafficking agencies for money."

"That's shocking," I had said with disgust. "I would never do that to Khin."

Ma Thet looked sad. "I guess people do horrible

things when faced with starvation."

It's a lot to ponder. No matter what I decide, I need to find work immediately. With only a third-grade education, my employment options are deplorable. I know that some women in the village find jobs doing road construction. However, I've also heard they're paid much less than the men performing the exact same tasks.

If I don't find a job, Khin won't be able to complete secondary school—she would need to work for household income until I could find work providing sufficient money. At eleven years old, she's just now finishing her first year of secondary school. She would be heartbroken to have to stop.

Some of the teenage girls in the village work at the garment factory down the road. Working conditions are appalling—bending over sewing machines for hours on end, surrounded by the constant hum of the machines and dust-filled air. Rumors fly around the village about girls disappearing from the factory, most likely victims of child trafficking. Their mamas and papas will probably never see their daughters again.

None of these scenarios sound safe or appealing. It's extremely overwhelming to think about. I don't even know how to budget money or use a bank account.

"Mama," murmurs Khin. "How is Papa this morning? Should I get some wood for the fire?" Drawing my blanket around me, I tiptoe over to her bed and kneel beside her. Wrapping her in a snug hug, I whisper softly, "Papa has left this life, dear Khin. He loved you very much. We will miss his hearty laugh and his funny stories. It will just be you and me now. My love for you is deeper than the ocean. Now we must be strong. Let's cook some rice for breakfast and visit the monk to make plans for Papa's viewing and funeral."

By the time we finished meeting with the monk and Aung's body was taken to the monastery for viewing, it was late afternoon. I longed to sit with my friends and drink my rich, malty, ink-black tea. I knew that Khin was eager to see her friends and tell them the news of her Papa's passing. With Ma Thet and Mu Mu, I knew I could speak freely, cry, laugh, or just be quiet in their company.

We call our friendship "women helping women." I see similar friendships between other women in the village. We openly share our feelings. We're not afraid to be vulnerable. We trust that our secrets and fears are safe with each other. And when we need help, whatever that might look like, we help each other—no questions asked. Sometimes I wonder what my life would be like without my women friends. It sounds empty, bleak, and lonely.

Grabbing my steaming cup of tea, I walk over to Mu Mu's home where she and Ma Thet are sitting on the porch. Having heard the news of Aung's passing, they immediately envelop me in their tender, loving hugs and don't let go of me until I am ready.

"How are you feeling? What can we do to help you? How is Khin taking this loss of her Papa?" asks Mu Mu.

"Even though Aung was ill for some time and

even though he was a burden to me many times, his loss creates a hole in my body where my heart used to be," I stutter. "Since I awoke this morning, my mind has been a jumble of worry about money, Khin's education, and whether or not I should remarry. Please give me advice, dear friends. My world is upside down, and I can't think straight."

"You know we will help you however you want and need," promises Ma Thet. "But first, we have learned some news that might solve all of our problems. Do you want to hear it now or would you like to sit and rest for a while first?"

"Oh, I need to hear good news. Tell me—what is it?"

"Our village elders have decided to coordinate with a microfinance organization to create a project here in Kamarnut. It will be for women!" exclaims Mu Mu. "A woman can apply to receive a $30 loan to create a small business here in the village. She will need to present a business plan to the elders, stating what she wants to do and why she believes it will be successful. If she is selected to participate, she will be taught how to manage the business and the money. She will have to pay a small interest rate, but most of that interest money will support our small grade school here in the village, attended by our young ones."

"There is a lot we still don't know about the project," said Ma Thet. "We think it might be an exciting opportunity to try. We know of another local village that's doing this. One woman whose home has electricity borrowed money to purchase a freezer. She lives next door to the government school and is now selling ice cream and popsicles to the children. Another woman borrowed money to start a bicycle repair business. She always enjoyed tinkering with bicycles to see how they are put together. And, as we know, all of our villages depend on bicycles. So her idea sounds like a good one! Another woman started a home shop, selling kitchen items, produce, rice, and coconut soup. She's taken out and repaid two loans and is now using her third loan to build her business even larger."

"Are you going to apply for loans?" I ask my friends. "What will your businesses be?"

"Yes!" Mu Mu and Ma Thet exclaim simultaneously.

"As you both know very well, I love beauty products and hair styling," says Mu Mu with a smile. "I want to open a beauty parlor. When a woman needs a haircut or make-up for her special day, she can come to my shop. I will make her look so beautiful!"

"And I will follow my dream to open a cigar-making business! I will pay young girls here in the village to help me make the tasty cheroots," smiles Ma Thet. "Daw Ni, are you also going to apply for a loan? What kind of business do you want?"

I'm interested, but not sure what my business could be. "The only thing I know I'm good at is making sticky rice," I say. "Do you think people in our village would buy it?"

"Oh definitely!" my friends exclaim. "It is mouth-watering heaven with every bite."

"Well," I declare, "if you are going to try it, so will I. Let's visit the elders and find out how to get started. I'm not sure what a business plan is, but I bet together we can figure it out."

Before we know it, Ma Thet, Mu Mu, and I have taken the first steps toward opening businesses and becoming independent women. We meet with the elders, learn about the application process, and begin writing our business plans. It's a flurry of activity and excitement, and a good distraction from Aung's passing and new widowhood.

Two weeks later, all three of us receive good news from the elders. We will each receive a $30 loan, with 2.5 percent interest. The interest monies will be directed back into the village community to support our village grade school and provide us with financial training in how to keep business records. If we successfully make our monthly loan payments on time, we will be able to apply for an additional $30 next year to expand our businesses.

I'd felt like my life turned upside down with Aung's passing, and now it was leading me on a new course—one that I never knew was possible. I had never thought about being independent, free to make decisions, able to provide for my daughter financially, and capable of being her role model.

If my sticky rice business is successful, Khin will be able to stay in secondary school. She won't have to work to earn money for us. I have always desired more for Khin's life—education to allow her to pursue her dreams, freedom to travel and meet new people, and confidence in herself to succeed in life.

Soon

Here I go! Today is the first day of my new business! I wake at dawn to make my first batch of sticky rice to sell. The texture is perfect—soft, sticky, sweet, and just the right amount of creamy coconut milk and mango juice. Melts in your mouth. I've decided to wear my favorite blue jacket covered with vibrant umbrellas for good luck. My big silver tray is full of sticky rice bites and ready to place securely on the soft towel on my head. I'll need to stand tall and walk like a statuesque model so the tray doesn't fall. I will call out as I walk through the village paths: "get your sticky rice here—a perfect breakfast bite—only 1 kyat per bite!"

I feel different today. I feel pretty and strong and determined. My face can't stop twisting into a huge grin. I think I am happy! I have decided to say a mantra to myself as I walk through the village.

May I stand tall with pride, a strong, self-sufficient woman able to make my own life decisions.

May I accept that I am powerful because I am a woman.

May my daughter become an educated, self-sufficient woman able to determine her future for herself.

I realize this is a huge turning point in my life. I won't have to remarry unless I choose to. I will learn many new skills, things I never in my wildest imagination could have conjured up. Living independently, I can decide for myself what I do, eat, say, or read. And the most wonderful part of this new path in my life is that I will be sharing it all with my women friends here in the village. I think "women helping women" is very formidable.

Khin is already very proud of me for starting my business. She believes that women need to try new things and take chances to see where it all leads. I think she is a very smart young woman already! We will learn from each other.

Alright, Daw Ni, off you go to sell your scrumptious sticky rice—stand tall with purpose and pride, and may the villagers be hungry!

Chapter 6
Burma 2021

Fast forward to February 1, 2021. The newly elected democratic majority was poised to take office, moving the country toward a legitimate democracy. Then, shockingly, the Burmese military junta once again closed its fist and took control. In the wee hours of the morning, the newly elected Burmese president and congressional leaders were rounded up and imprisoned. The internet was shut down and cell service ceased.

Sitting on the other side of the world, watching the news, I wept with disbelief and anguish. With the current state of our world, in the middle of an ongoing global pandemic, I knew no substantive assistance would be provided by the West. We were already stretched thin on too many other fronts. I felt helpless and fraught with worry for the safety and future of my Burmese partners and friends.

The Burmese people's reaction was immediate. They had tasted freedom and connected globally with other freedom fighters. They had learned how to rapidly mobilize a civil disobedience movement. Their technology expertise by that point was advanced, allowing them to circumvent the military junta's attempts to stifle internet and cell phone communications. Throughout the country, rural and city residents protested and clogged traffic to impact commerce. Although they had no access to sophisticated weapons, they began converting whatever was available to protect themselves.

Even though the people were willing and able to fight this latest military junta control measure, their lives were significantly and immediately disrupted. They were strong. But still afraid and confused.

Over previous decades, the Burmese had continued to demonstrate the power of the human spirit to maintain hope for a better life. Would they be able to withstand this latest attempt to snuff out their independence?

I knew my ability to empower Burmese women with education was indefinitely suspended. The military junta was burning villages to the ground throughout the country. The number of displaced people grew daily. Basics such as food and clothing became desperate needs.

Educational Empowerment's regular means of transferring funds into the country were either unavailable or insecure. I sought a way to help outside my normal channels, but once again was not sure where to begin. Unexpectedly, a Burmese friend who had immigrated to the United States many years prior reached out to me for assistance. She wanted to help her family and friends back home but wasn't sure how to do it. The next day on Facebook I saw a posting about a Burmese restaurant opening in Seattle, the first ever. Another coincidence, or not? I immediately called the owner to introduce myself, suggesting that we three women coordinate to raise funds for displaced people inside Burma. She readily agreed.

Simultaneously, I pursued options to transfer the donations into Burma that would ensure they reached those most in need. I connected with a well-established nonprofit organization in the United States that had an extensive on-the-ground network inside Burma. With their assistance, we were able to transfer money raised at our fundraising event directly to displaced families in Burma.

Unfortunately, there was little else I was able to do at the time. Covid restrictions and an unexpected personal health trauma put my life on a significant hold. I continued to be an active presence in the lives of my friends and partners in Burma, wanting desperately for them to know they were not forgotten, however, I knew they couldn't speak freely in emails or on social media, because their movements and communications were constantly monitored. And I couldn't travel to Burma to see them in person.

As of 2024, the Burmese military junta continues to rule the land amidst its reign of terror. The Burmese haven't given up their desire for democracy, but time, lack of international assistance, and their sinking economy have taken a toll.

Women struggle to protect and feed their children. Dreams of equal access to education have been all but extinguished. Without their homes and villages, families are once again forced to seek refuge in the jungles. Without the farmers' crops, food is scarce for everyone. Medical assistance is unattainable. Escape across borders is dangerous due to landmines planted by the military junta. Humanitarian aid is stifled by the military junta's roadblocks and its theft of supplies.

The country has stepped back in time to 2010. This time it is almost more heartbreaking—the Burmese people know about the world, but their access to it has been taken from them once again.

The Choice

The skies are aglow with shimmers of pink petals, signaling the break of dawn, as if this is just an ordinary day. My pounding heart and twitching fingers warn me otherwise. Only one more banner to secure across Bogyoke Aung San Road. One more longyi to hang to protect our protest zone. These soldiers will be disgusted to walk beneath our long skirts. They shudder to be close to clothing worn by a "dirty" female body, risking their spiritual manhood. This longyi banner will stop traffic and impact commerce. We do whatever we can with whatever we have to stop their movements.

Hurry, hurry my mind chants. I finish the job and don my hard hat and vest. We never know when the shooting might start, disrupting our peaceful protest. Thousands are expected today.

Was it really just last month, in the dark of night, that the military junta again tightened its fists? They imprisoned the President and Aung San Suu Kyi, our beacon of hope for democracy, whom we affectionately call The Lady. They shut down the internet. Cell phone service ceased. And our country returned, once again, to the blackout we'd known for fifty years.

A few weeks prior to the coup, I sat in my university business class, taking my final exam. I was eager to apply for a Master's Degree program with an emphasis on minority-owned businesses. Life was filled with hope and opportunities. My phone connected me to the outside world. I could safely walk a street, trusting that eye contact with strangers held no betrayal. The taste of freedom was ripe in my mouth.

I dreamt of being a changemaker and a role model for girls. The world was at my feet. Vivid dreams of possibilities filled my mind. Mama and Papa had already moved on to their reborn lives, seeking Nirvana. Without worries, I would care for Kyi Kyi, my teenage sister, affectionately called Nan as the younger one. Nan would thrive in a world without fear or violence. She would rise above poverty and embody hope for our country.

All my life I have been fearless and determined. Mama used to call me her intrepid peanut. When I asked her why, she said proudly, "You are tiny, but you are brave. You are a superhero who seeks truth and justice." Her words gave me confidence that still runs deep in my soul.

Today I will be intrepid. I will stand tall and let my voice be heard for democracy. When darkness falls, I will join my neighbors with pots and pans at the ready to warn of danger. But now, I must finish the banner and locate my protest spot.

Positioned near Bogyoke Market, on the outer edge of the protestors, I scan the crowd for police, soldiers, and suspect men. There must be hundreds of women here today, and the noise level from all the nervous chatter is unbearable. The air is thick with humidity, making it difficult to take a breath. Heat already dampening my clothes. It will only worsen as the sun rises.

Even though our gathering is peaceful, the military junta rarely maintains restraint. Women are easy targets for manhandling, threats, and yanking off clothing to reveal breasts. All protestors are targets for imprisonment and death. I must remain vigilant.

Soon, Aung San Road is overflowing with women chanting "No to dictatorship! No to patriarchy!" Traffic is stalled. Businesses are closed. We feed off each other's passion and commitment.

Suddenly, I feel someone press against me. A male voice in my ear whispers sexual debasements and threats, things I have never before heard. A hand slips under my longyi. I scream and turn to face my assailant. He slaps my face, and I know I am no match for his aggressiveness. I must flee. Pushing through the crowd in front of me, I run as best I can. Women behind me close ranks to protect my path even though they aren't sure what causes me to flee. I continue to run. I continue on, screaming my horror.

I think back to the peacefulness of my childhood growing up in Shan State. The hilly plateau's sunny climate was ideal for Mama and Papa to grow an abundance of fruits and vegetables. They easily sold their produce at the traveling markets that moved from village to village. Kyi Kyi and I tagged along to help and meet new friends. She and I were always play fighting, with little jabs, tickles, and merciless tripping of each other. One time I made eye contact with her, and she asked "why are you looking at me? do you want to fight?" I was in a good mood that day. So, I said "you are so beautiful when you chatter/chatter." She still pushed me in the face laughing. "Please wash your face before you go to bed tonight, big sister. I am afraid of your ghost face." And she chased me across the field.

At that time, the military junta had no interest in education, and books for children didn't exist. Folktale stories shared around the fire each night provided our entertainment. The story of how Inle Lake came to be was my favorite.

As the story goes, there used to be four small lakes in a wide-open field. A resident monster loved to eat the fish. But he needed more water in the lakes for the fish to thrive and feed his appetite. The monster dug a falling stream. It flew into the field, flooding the small lakes and creating a single vast magnificent lake.

One day the monster caught the King Fish and readily devoured him. The King Fish turned into a powerful spirit god—what we call a Nat. As a Nat spirit, he now held the power. With a flutter of his wings, he turned the monster into a miniature stick insect.

Then the Nat spirit caught hundreds more insects and piled them high on the stick insect, topping the pile with mud, sand, rubbish, dead leaves, and seeds. These piles became mountains. Plants and trees thrived in the rich, insect-fertilized soil. Wildlife sought out this new lush paradise. Humans followed to build their villages. Inle Lake was born.

I always found this story's happy ending and sense of hope in the face of evil inspirational. I loved that justice prevailed, and the evil monster got his comeuppance.

Now, I see it as a symbol for hope in the face of war and destruction. I hope Kyi Kyi and I can learn from this example, illustrating that life and beauty can thrive and prevail, even in the face of monsters.

Growing up in Shan State there was always danger from the military junta's random assaults, but for the most part, the hills protected us. Our existence felt secure and idyllic.

Our village school provided an education not available to most children, especially girls. Mama and Papa knew the importance of education to attaining our dreams. Educating us was their priority.

As I get closer to home, I tell myself to focus. I need to plan what to say to Nan when I arrive.

Over the past month of protesting, I've seen how peaceful civil disobedience can quickly erupt into violence. Today's assault reminded me that, despite being an intrepid young women, we are vulnerable. I promised Mama and Papa I would protect Kyi Kyi. I will fulfill that commitment. I'm just not sure what it looks like these days.

Since the coup, all Burmese people face similar decisions. Thousands have been displaced. The military junta burns villages and plants landmines to deter a return to crop fields. Many people live in makeshift camps with no ability to grow food or earn income to feed their children. The economy continues to worsen. The Covid pandemic runs rampant, with no availability of vaccines or care. The future is bleak.

Some have chosen to join the ethnic state armies, fighting for their rights and defending themselves. Others have chosen makeshift homes in the jungle. Still others have abandoned our homeland, leaving their families and crossing borders to seek safety in Laos, China, or Thailand. Some have simply ignored the reality of our country's demise.

I have spent countless sleepless nights considering options for Nan and me. My greatest fear is loss of freedom. Freedom to attain an education. Freedom to attain my rights and make my own decisions—where to live, whom to marry. Freedom from violence. Freedom to speak my mind without fear of repercussion.

Jungle life is not freedom. It is persecution and a temporary escape from violence.

Becoming a soldier for Shan State Army is not freedom. Although women are accepted into battle, they take their orders from men. They do not make decisions.

Ignoring our country's authoritarian dictatorship is foolhardy. The military junta is a greedy, controlling mob of men who will not give away power soon or easily.

Escaping to Laos or China only trades one dictatorship for another. Thailand is the only option for us. We will travel alone. As two girls, we will draw less attention than a large family group.

Hope still shines bright in my heart. Mama taught me that we must let go of the old when faced with change. We must plant our new garden. We must step into the dark abyss of the unknown and brighten it with our light. Her teachings strengthen my confidence for this escape.

Finally, I am home at our dilapidated apartment on the outskirts of Yangon. We were fortunate to find a place to live in this small township. We have a kitchen and indoor toilet and nearby neighbors looking out for each other. And we have electricity, not available to everyone in our country.

When I open the front door, I see Kyi Kyi busily cooking. She's sixteen years old already. Such a beautiful young woman with her big brown eyes and lustrous black hair. She takes after Mama. Unfortunately, I look more like Papa with my fair hair and stocky build.

Kyi Kyi's face is smudged all over with spices. Our tiny kitchen doesn't provide much room for tidy cooking. But she looks happy. Unfortunately, I know that joy will change when we talk over dinner. I know my disheveled appearance and grim face will convey my distress. I won't share details of my assault yet. Those conversations will have to wait for later.

"Nan, my mouth is watering and my stomach is grumbling like an elephant from the smell of your noodles. Let's eat."

As we sit together at our tiny table, I begin to tell her my thoughts. "The time has come for us to leave our country for safety and freedom. Life here has become as fragile as a lotus blossom. We're both strong, but we're also vulnerable to the evil out there. That military junta is smothering our dreams."

"What do you mean, Hla Mae? You're scaring me!" my little sister quivers.

"We need to leave Yangon, and return to the mountains we know. I believe our best hope for a good life lies in Thailand. We'll need to be brave in the forests before crossing the mighty peak of Loi Leng. We might not be welcome in Thailand. We won't know their language or customs. We'll be leaving our homeland and friends for an unknown world. But if we trust our Buddhist beliefs, we'll find a place of strength within. Will you trust me again, Nan, as you did when we moved to Yangon?" Her nodding head says yes. Her grim expression says fear.

"Okay then. Let's pack our most treasured possessions. We'll leave at dawn to travel north, deep into the Shan mountains. While we're on the bus, I will explain to you why I believe this is our best choice for safety and freedom."

That night, Kyi Kyi thoughtfully selects her treasured copy of I Am Malala, her favorite photo of Mama and Papa, sturdy walking shoes, and clothing to keep her warm in the frigid mountainous temperatures. But how do you fit all your life's keepsakes and essentials into one small knapsack?

We curled together in our bed, sleeping with the heaviness of approaching dawn. We have always been a comfort to each other. And we trust each other to speak freely. I have loved her fiercely since I first held her in my arms right after her birth.

At the bus station, we grab bread and bananas. The bus provides us with water and dental kits. Our thirteen-hour journey on bumpy curvy roads begins.

Neither of us is able to sleep on the bus thanks to cackling chickens, crying babies, blaring music, and the overwhelming magnitude of our decision.

Arriving in Taunggyi, we glimpse Inle Lake, prompting memories of traveling markets, floating villages, and the mysterious leg rowers of the long boats.

We find a small room for the night and once again devour Shan noodles before falling into a deep slumber.

Dawn's glow and mouth-watering scents wake us early. Our trek to Loi Leng will be fraught with danger, requiring fourteen hours on foot through dense forests riddled with landmines planted by both Shan militias and the military junta, and rolling highland meadows, fertile territory for deadly airstrikes. Ever-present soldiers, assault rifles at the ready to shoot indiscriminately at civilians.

As we eat our breakfast by the fire, Kyi Kyi's trusting, brave smile reminds me of our strong bond, built through adversity and shared loss. When Mama passed from fever five years ago, Kyi Kyi was a young girl. Moving forward after Mama's death was horrendous. The farm required constant physical labor and unlearned skills. Our young bodies suffered from the unending bending and lifting. We quickly understood the burdens Mama had carried.

Papa never recovered. He turned to palm wine for his escape. The responsibility for growing and selling the crops fell upon us girls.

Then Papa caught the Covid virus. His frail body and lack of will to live took him from us quickly. Sadly, his karma at the moment of death would make his journey to Nirvana long with endless suffering. Our only choice was to leave the farm and move to Yangon to seek education. As with this choice to leave our country, Kyi Kyi trusted me to make the right decision, and she was happy in Yangon.

Alone in the world, we were inseparable. Kyi

Kyi's laughter shined a golden light on the most difficult of days. My steady course and determination built a safety net for her fears. Words were not needed. Simple gestures and expressions became our communication. We prayed this bond would serve us well in our life ahead.

"Little Nan, can you do this? Will you go with me to Thailand?" I whisper.

"I think I can, Pi," she responds, showing respect for me as elder sister. "I will try BIG!" Her bravado swells my heart with pride. Gripping hands, we valiantly stride into the forest, both full of hope.

Campfire remnants and crude tarpaulin shelters scattered among the trees provide immediate evidence of the many displaced people, like us, fleeing Burma. With eyes on alert and ears open to voices or gunshots, we begin the gradual ascent up Loi Leng, highest peak in Shan State. At 9,000 feet, its crest separates Burma from Thailand, where we will first lay eyes on our new homeland.

After several hours, our bodies cry for nourishment and a brief rest. We sit in silence on boulders overlooking Inle Lake, thinking of the Nat spirit who filled these mountains with life. We quench our thirst and nibble fruit. A woman's voice alerts us to other travelers slowly approaching. We soon see a small boy struggling up the hillside, followed by his parents. With relief, we know they are not our enemies.

Our fellow travelers stop to rest with us. They speak of their village in the valley being burnt to ashes by the soldiers and their quick flight with the few belongings they could carry.

They tell us of makeshift schools they saw in the jungle. Classes held under trees with teachers using rocks and charcoal for blackboards. Lessons taught by older students or adults with minimal educational training.

They tell us of vivid images embedded in their eyes: abandoned weapons, charred ruins, discarded housewares and children's toys. With hushed voices, they share stories of landmine accident deaths and lost limbs. They saw the wounded being treated in an outdoor jungle clinic. Shaky operating tables and a dispensary fashioned out of bamboo strips. One resistant militia member rested on a wooden platform, his leg bandaged from a gunshot wound sustained in fighting last month. Apparently, eight other fighters were injured that very day. Their words fill our minds with terror.

Still, they knew this to be their only choice offering hope. And we are so very close now.

Kyi Kyi and I resume our journey, leaving our fellow travelers to enjoy precious moments of peace.

As the climbing becomes more challenging, our breath runs ragged and our pace slows noticeably. Within a couple hours, we see crop fields and haphazard dwellings. Women hang laundry. Children chase each other, squealing with delight. Men stack firewood. And Shan Army militia fighters, with weapons slung across their bodies, wander to and fro. This village is Loi Tai Leng, a displaced-person camp for those now homeless. Residents receive some protection from the military junta as the Shan Army is located here. I know that similar displaced person camps lay scattered all around our country.

"Pi, is this Thailand?" Kyi Kyi's smile is filled with excitement.

"Almost, little Nan. But let's walk on a bit further. Not too far though. We will be able to catch the first glimpse of our new home. Mama's and Papa's hearts must be bursting with love and pride for your incredible strength. I hope you know how proud of you I am—always! Please watch where you walk though. We are not yet safe."

Many of the men at Loi Tai Leng have lost a leg or an arm, and many women are widowed due to landmine explosions. I know that landmines are easy to make and difficult to see when planted in the ground. Frequently, children see something sticking out of the dirt. They pull at it, out of curiosity, and it explodes. It is heartrending.

We will not be out of harm's way until we are inside Thailand.

As we continue to Loi Leng's crest, we spot a grove of lush orange mangoes. Our grumbling stomachs urge us to savor one last prized fruit. We both giggle with visions of mango juice dripping from our chins.

Before I can stop her, Kyi Kyi runs toward the closest tree.

"No, Nan, come back to me," I shout. Yet, she

does not stop. Maybe she doesn't hear me? Maybe her ears are ringing with mango dreams? I watch her with gaping mouth. It is as if she is running in slow motion. She looks so beautiful and innocent. My heart pounds with fear. Maybe she will be safe? I need my little Nan. We are a team. We complete each other's world. I don't want this moment to be her time.

Kyi Kyi reaches the mango tree. I breathe with relief and gratitude. All is well.

Suddenly, the ground beneath her erupts into billowing black smoke. The bomb's shock wave releases an expanding sphere of hot gas. Hot metal fragments fill the sky.

"NO!! NO!!" erupts a roar from the depths of my soul. "NO!!"

I see the remains of her ravaged body sprawled under the tree. I can't believe what I see. We are so near to the crest.

"Nan, what have I done to you? How can I go on without you? I wish it would have been me," I utter as sorrow sweeps through my body and tears cascade down my face like small electric shocks.

I know immediately she is gone, awaiting a reborn life.

My heart knows that I must move forward for her.

Kyi Kyi wouldn't want me to falter. She would want me to achieve the freedom I seek—for her, for Mama, and for Papa. I must continue my search for freedom—to attain my education, my rights, and my ability to make my own decisions; to be free from violence; and to speak my mind without fear.I know she will either return as a human or a Nat spirit, because she was happy at the last minute of her life. I need to remember her as the vibrant little sister I cherish. I do not want my last vision of her to be that shattered physical shell.

I slowly continue walking.

"I choose to live this life fearlessly and abundantly," I chant over and over again as I continue to the crest, tears streaming down my face and sobs echoing throughout my body.

Oh, dear Nan, I will love you forever.

Chapter 7
Reflections

Dry season. A swath of land cleared to the bone as if a rumbling giant has recklessly scuttled past. In its wake, quiet, time standing still, mind calming. A brief respite to ponder.

Did Hla Mae finally achieve the freedom she sought in Thailand? Did Daw Ni soar with newly attained self-confidence and self-reliance? Did Pawlin find solace and strength through her support for victims of abuse? Did Maiah rejoice through her empowerment of girls and boys in the Delta? Did Aye Sander and Thiri find contentment in their lives as nuns? Did Nang attain peace while hiking in the Cascade mountains of Washington State?

As Parker J. Palmer describes so eloquently in his poem Everything Falls Away—we follow, unknowingly, the thread we didn't know we were taking until everything else falls away.

Reflecting on my life of seventy-six years, I see a continuum of transformation, as I have grown from passive observer to active changemaker; from a shy young woman, unable to speak thoughts aloud, to a confident vocal advocate for women's rights.

Looking back at myself when serving as City of Seattle's Procurement Director, I remember frequently being unable to speak out and express my opinions. Even though I was well respected in a high-level position, I often reverted to the shy young girl unable to speak her thoughts aloud.

Confidence in oneself takes time to build and to maintain. Although I was more confident than in my earlier years, I continued to question whether my opinion mattered. Could I speak eloquently in a meeting or would I stutter? Would others listen to me? I had the thoughts, but not the courage nor the confidence to speak up. Yes, I could create change, but could I sell it?

My efforts to support women and girls in Burma are heartfelt. When speaking from my heart, my confidence is resolute. I know my actual words are not as important as my passion and commitment to doing all I can to help these people who stole my heart.

Age is also a factor when learning to speak aloud. At age seventy-six what do I have to lose?

Writing about my life has been an opportunity to identify patterns and connections of events, relationships, and decisions. I now see that steps I took during my life were not necessarily random actions, but paths leading to self-discovery and my life's passion. Some of the paths I chose were easy to see and follow. Sometimes I did not listen to my gut and chose the wrong path. And with Educational Empower, I created my path.

As I learned from my brief connection to the Burmese woman in Bagan, I have always been drawn to learning of and from other women. My work in Burma empowering women to achieve their rights and live free of abuse and degradation has turned out to be the passion I'd been seeking unknowingly. In hindsight, I wish I had seen it earlier.

We women are a gift to each other. A dear friend in her nineties is a constant inspiration to me. She is wise, funny, smart, and actively demonstrates how to live life to the fullest till the end. She encourages me to write the stories in my heart. She tells me how thankful she is for our friendship. I relish her wisdom and guidance.

My eightyish-year-old women friends teach me how to thoughtfully and selectively maintain independence, the importance of an active sense of humor, especially as the body slowly crumbles, and the strength of our minds to maintain functionality.

Simultaneously, dear women friends in their fifties and sixties tell me how I inspire them with positivity, wisdom, and energy. To them, I demonstrate that life doesn't halt when you reach seventy. There is still much to learn, see, and do, especially in service of others.

My friend Mercy, who just turned fifty, is a Burmese American who immigrated to the United States when she was eighteen. Her strength enabled her to rise above an unexpected divorce and subsequent single-parenting of her two children.

Now a passionate advocate for quality education for minority children, she is applying for admittance to the University of Washington for a Master's Degree in Language, Literacy, and Culture. She intends to advocate for education opportunities for all children. She credits her determination to continue following new paths to being inspired by me. Although I know in my heart that she would have found these strengths on her own, I feel immense gratitude to think I might have helped her along in her journey.

This cross-generational guidance and role modeling represents the strength of women's relationships.

When we speak openly, from our hearts, without fear or embarrassment, others tend to respond with like openness and honesty. When this happens, it's a powerful and fulfilling connection. We learn from each other and laugh together. For me, this validates my decades-long fascination with the deep friendships of which we women are capable.

I wish that more men would build and enjoy connections with their male friends. I've been told many times that my husband is unique because his male friends openly confide in him. I'm immensely proud of him for his ability to be vulnerable and to enable other men to follow suit.

The power and beauty of my relationships with women, especially with my daughter Tatiana, became vividly evident to me during my recent illness and diagnosis of an incurable lung disease.

In 2021, after being ill for six months, with increasingly reduced lung capacity, I received a diagnosis of Idiopathic Pulmonary Fibrosis (IPF), a progressive and ultimately terminal disease. Suddenly, I was reminded that I was mortal.

Over the next six months I struggled to process this unanticipated news. Having been blessedly healthy all my life, I wasn't familiar with health-related limitations. Always an independent and active person, I found struggling to walk up a flight of stairs or the aisles of the grocery store disconcerting at best. Vulnerability and dependence on others was a new concept to me. It was humbling to walk in the shoes of the many people living with health and mobility limitations.

My family and dear friends surrounded me with love and support. I learned from them how to help others in pain. I learned that a simple text letting me know a friend was thinking of me brought immense comfort. I learned that providing updates on my status was exhausting. I learned to be thankful for every breath.

Navigating the medical and insurance systems was time-intensive and frustrating. Finally connecting with a real person on the phone after an extended wait time was a halleluiah moment. Always a strong advocate for myself, I knew how to be assertive without being overhanded but my heart broke for those unable to do the same for themselves or those without family to serve as advocates.

I accepted my shortened mortality prognosis reasonably well. We all die at some point, and my time was just coming sooner than expected. Thankful for the rich life I have lived, I didn't want to waste my remaining time on self-pity.

The most difficult aspect was seeing the pain in the eyes of my family and friends. It is easier to be the one dying than the one left behind.

Prior to my illness, I had come to think of myself as intrepid—adventurous, dauntless, willing to take risks. After my diagnosis, a dear friend gifted me a small silver heart. The word intrepid was engraved on the back.

This reminded me that the women of Burma are intrepid. And the paths they take in life to attain their rights and values are fraught with unknown events and choices. This was an inspirational lightbulb moment for me—to entitle my story collection Intrepid Paths—Burma. And to earnestly move forward with writing and sharing these women's stories.

Shortly after my diagnosis, I was admitted to the care of Dr. Raghu, a world-renowned expert in IPF at University of Washington. Unbeknownst to me, he questioned whether my diagnosis was accurate, as it is a difficult disease to identify. He prescribed a couple of medications for me for the following three-month period, knowing that if I did have IPF, the drugs would have no impact on my condition. However, if I did not have IPF, the drugs might significantly clear up my lungs.

At my next appointment, I received another CT scan and pulmonary function test. When I saw the results, my jaw dropped! The majority of the "permanent" scar tissue in my lungs had disappeared. The drugs which Dr. Raghu had given me had cleared up the inflammation in my lungs before it became solidified into permanent scar tissue. After living with a death sentence for six months, I was literally given a new lease on life, air flowing freely through my lungs with each breath.

If not for my doctor's expertise, I would have unknowingly continued on whilst the inflammation in my lungs turned to hardened scar tissue and my ability to breathe worsened.

Although I still have a minor lung disease created by environmental and autoimmune factors, it's not progressively terminal and is being controlled very well with non-invasive drugs.

My prior medical team members were accredited personnel. My pulmonologist, surgeon, and pathologist had poured over my lung biopsy results and together made a thoughtful diagnosis of IPF. I have no ill feelings toward them or their skills. However, Dr. Raghu is the expert. I will eternally be grateful to him and to the University of Washington for saving me.

It took me a few weeks to process this major change in my lifespan. When I told family and friends about this mini miracle, they literally rejoiced. One friend explained her reaction well. She had been grieving for me even though I was still alive. With my news, she felt a weight lifted from her heart. She didn't have to worry about bad news with every phone call. She could relax and enjoy her life, as well as mine.

I am rich in thankfulness—for my outstanding and intuitive doctor, for my ability to breath freely again, for every beautiful morning, and for the outpouring of love surrounding me.

While I rejoice in the knowledge that my mortality is at bay for a bit longer, death is a battle we all lose eventually—some sooner than others. My amazing friend Denise, having just turned sixty years old, passed away last week after battling cancer for over three years. A woman of faith, she wasn't afraid to die. However, while still able to speak, her last words to me expressed her regret for wasting her past few years fighting death. Those years were fraught with excruciating impacts from chemotherapy and autoimmune drug regimens, loss of weight, and inability to perform once-normal life functions. She desperately loved her family and wanted to stay alive for them, but in hindsight, she wished that she had just lived the life she had left. She asked me to tell others, faced with similar decisions, to seriously weigh their options and to choose life quality over quantity. May she rest in peace.

I intend to live my remaining years with purpose. For me, this means continuing to create awareness of Burma and its people, truly living every moment, celebrating life and my family and friends, and giving back to others as much as possible.

Unable to continue projects in Burma due to its unstable military junta-controlled environment, I have turned to assisting local Burmese immigrants as they navigate life in the United States. Financial skills and an awareness of available options within our government's systems are necessary to become self-reliant. These are intelligent, strong women who only need a bit of guidance and encouragement to soar.

As a testament to the power of the human spirit to maintain hope, the Burmese people have made positive progress in attempting to regain control of their country.

On Oct. 27, 2023, an alliance of three different ethnic armed organizations, known as the Three Brotherhood Alliance, launched a surprise offensive that overwhelmed the military junta across Burma's northern border with China. These forces, comprised of ragtag revolutionaries and well-equipped battle-hardened soldiers, had never before collaborated for the benefit of their shared democratic aspirations.

Simultaneously, the military junta's morale has disintegrated. Some experts, sensing that the tide is turning, believe it could lead to the military junta's disintegration.

Others worry that such a collapse might not lead to peace. Lacking a common enemy, the coalition of leaders from the exiled democratic shadow government and the ethnic militias could easily disintegrate again into rival groups, foolishly turning their guns on each other.

I, for one, urge the United States and other international democracy proponents to officially recognize and support the National Unity Government—to begin serious conversations in preparation for logistical measures to be implemented in support of the people's tangible opportunity for democracy.

Timing is crucial. At least 5,000 women have been arrested by the military junta since the 2021 coup. They have suffered cruel, degrading treatment, including sexual assault, denial of water or medical treatment, and torture. Their families don't know whether they are alive or dead. Their crime is "opposition via peaceful protest." Displacement of women and children has reached record highs. Starvation runs rampant.

Being a person of optimism, I see hope for this country I love. It's time for Burmese people to have their day in the light. Yet, time will tell whether that hope comes to fruition.

Moving forward with my new lease on life, I have an opportunity to earnestly strive to be a better person.

I am fortunate to be alive. I have a precious human life. I am not going to waste it. I am going to use all my energies to develop myself, to expand my heart out to others. I am going to have kind thoughts towards others. I am not going to get angry or think badly about others. I am going to benefit others as much as I can.

—"A Precious Human Life" by Dalai Lama XIV

Understanding that this is an admirable goal, I'm not foolish enough to believe it will be easy. Yet, I do intend to try.

There's no reason to wait, no reason to hold back, no reason to quiet my voice. I intend to speak openly from my heart. Age doesn't have to be a limiting factor when exploring new growth and choices. I look forward to seeking opportunities in my years ahead to enrich my life and the lives of others.

There is always more life to live and new adventures to explore. Intrepid Paths is my first step in that direction.

Acknowledgments

Sincere thanks to my editor, Jacoba Lawson, for your outstanding skills, good eye, insights, and extraordinary patience.

Aye Myat Thu, your design creativity for Intrepid Paths' book cover, capturing the essence of my message, brings me to tears. Heartfelt thanks to you.

To my husband Michael and daughter Tatiana, thank you for always listening to me rattle on, encouraging me, and loving me. What would I do without you.

And endless gratitude to my dear friends and sister for your ongoing patience with my obsession throughout this process and for your continued encouragement.

Image Credits

Images on pages 6 and 120 available via public domain.

All other images created by the author.

Page 6—2022	*Burma 2022 Ethnic States Map*
Page 7 —2011	*After departing the train in Yangon, a woman carries greens to morning market for sale*
Page 27—2011	*Mon mother and children chat with friends*
Page 48—2012	*Novice nuns enjoy a moment together at Yangon nunnery*
Page 70—2015	*Brother and sister walk across Delta fields to school*
Page 86—2014	*Girl sells fruit at Inle Lake traveling market*
Page 100—2014	*Microfinance loan recipients and I gather together in village*
Page 120—2021	*The Spring Revolution's call to protest*